"S...

M... ... you mean.

"About us. This dating fiasco we've gotten ourselves into."

"We can pull it off. We may have to kiss, but you didn't mind my kisses the night of the Christmas party, did you? Surely you could tolerate a few more."

He smiled devilishly, and Kristi's heart fluttered. She had enjoyed his kisses. "Uh, they were okay," she said.

"Just okay?" Mitch's grin widened as he recognized her lie. "We'll have to work on that."

"Oh, that's not necessary," Kristi began, but Mitch's mouth lowered anyway....

Dear Reader,

I must confess—I love office romances. Not that I work in an office. But I love writing these types of stories because the tension between two people who are forbidden to fall in love—because they have a job to do—is just such a fun dynamic to work with. Do they break the rules? Do they risk their careers? Can they have it all?

Kristi Jensen doesn't think so. She's the romantically challenged daughter of the CEO, and she's clueless that her personal assistant, the very sexy Mitch Robbins, has loved her from afar for the past two years. Mitch could probably change Kristi's bad dating karma and provide the sparks missing from her life, if only she wasn't his boss. If only she didn't think he was in love with someone else. When Kristi discovers she's pregnant, their romance, and the office, will never be the same.

Baby in the Boardroom was a true treat to write. Mitch and Kristi constantly surprised me. Love is often about setting aside your fears, truly communicating and being ready to risk everything—even if it means you might fail. Doing the right thing is not as easy as it sounds. Luckily there's always a happy ending.

I hope you enjoy reading *Baby in the Boardroom* as much as I enjoyed creating it. Feel free to contact me by visiting www.micheledunaway.com or finding my page on Facebook. And as always, enjoy the romance.

Michele

Baby in
the Boardroom

MICHELE DUNAWAY

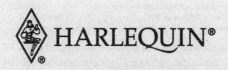

HARLEQUIN®

TORONTO • NEW YORK • LONDON
AMSTERDAM • PARIS • SYDNEY • HAMBURG
STOCKHOLM • ATHENS • TOKYO • MILAN • MADRID
PRAGUE • WARSAW • BUDAPEST • AUCKLAND

Recycling programs
for this product may
not exist in your area.

ISBN-13: 978-0-373-75297-3

BABY IN THE BOARDROOM

www.eHarlequin.com

Printed in U.S.A.

ABOUT THE AUTHOR

In first grade Michele Dunaway knew she wanted to be a teacher when she grew up, and by second grade she knew she wanted to be an author. By third grade she was determined to be both, and before her high school class reunion, she'd succeeded. In addition to writing romance, Michele is a nationally recognized English and journalism educator who also advises both the yearbook and newspaper at her school. Born and raised in a west county suburb of St. Louis, Missouri, Michele has traveled extensively, with the cities and places she's visited often becoming settings for her stories. Described as a woman who does too much but doesn't ever want to stop, Michele gardens five acres in her spare time and shares her house with two young daughters and five extremely lazy house cats and one rambunctious kitten that rule the roost.

Books by Michele Dunaway

HARLEQUIN AMERICAN ROMANCE

988—THE PLAYBOY'S PROTÉGÉE
1008—ABOUT LAST NIGHT…
1044—UNWRAPPING MR. WRIGHT
1056—EMERGENCY ENGAGEMENT
1100—LEGALLY TENDER
1116—CAPTURING THE COP
1127—THE MARRIAGE CAMPAIGN*
1144—THE WEDDING SECRET*
1158—NINE MONTHS' NOTICE*
1191—THE CHRISTMAS DATE
1207—THE MARRIAGE RECIPE
1251—TWINS FOR THE TEACHER
1265—BACHELOR CEO

*American Beauties

This book is for all my former students
and my high school classmates
with whom I've reconnected on Facebook.
Here's to technology. Cheers!

Chapter One

She was being dumped. Kristi Jensen collapsed against the back of her chair. The usual clatter of the Thai restaurant faded away as she stared at Bill. "I don't think I heard you correctly."

"I'm leaving you," her boyfriend of a year repeated. He twisted his fork in the ginger sauce-covered noodles, either oblivious or unconcerned about his words' impact. "We've had a good run and you'll always be special to me, but I met someone at my brother's bachelor party and I'm in love."

"You're in love?"

His eyes got dreamy.

"Yeah. Love. Not that I didn't love you, but this is different. She's twenty-one, hot and she makes my blood boil. I swear there were actual sparks. It was love at first sight." Bill emphasized his point by waving his fork before he dug in for one more bite.

"Uh-huh," Kristi replied, her appetite fading fast.

"Surely you knew things weren't working out between us."

Actually, she'd thought they'd been fine. Their relationship had never been especially passionate, but he'd fit her lifestyle. They were comfortable and compatible. And her parents had liked him. She'd thought he was getting ready to pop the question.

Now Kristi saw that the sports car Bill had purchased a month ago had been the beginning of a midlife crisis. He was dumping her for someone fourteen years his junior—barely old enough to legally drink. Love. Ha. Please.

Unable to help herself, Kristi asked, "So was she a guest at the party?"

"No, the stripper," Bill answered, not missing a bite. "But she's stripping only to make money to pay for college. It's not like she works on the East Side. She's much more professional than that. Just private parties. I told her when we're married she needs to quit. It's not like I can't support her."

"How nice." Bill's uptight, nose-in-the-air mother was going to be simply thrilled when she met her new daughter-in-law-to-be.

But that wasn't Kristi's problem. Her relationship with the man was clearly over. She pushed her plate forward and took a ten-dollar bill out of her purse. Tossing the money on the table, she prepared to leave.

Bill glanced around, as if appearances suddenly mattered. "Kristi, please. Don't walk out. Finish your lunch. They know us here. And it's not like I slept with you after I slept with her."

Kristi, long accustomed to having her relationships fail for one reason or another, held on to the last vestiges of shredded pride. "Well, isn't that special. At least I won't catch anything."

Somehow managing not to wobble in her two-inch pumps, she got to her feet. She would not cry. She refused to shed one tear over Bill, or mourn the time she'd wasted thinking he was the one.

She smoothed a wrinkle in her skirt and grabbed her coat. Then, without saying another word, she walked out, leaving Bill and the future she thought they would share behind.

"Damn," she cursed as she climbed into her car. The company Christmas party was tonight and her parents were going to be highly disappointed when she told them the news. Kristi Jensen, only child of the founder and CEO of the largest beer distributor in the Midwest, was dateless yet again. She gritted her teeth. She had a million things to take care of before the end of the day. She would lose herself in work, put off the pity party until tomorrow. She had a job to do.

MITCH ROBBINS PACED the carpet in front of his desk, stopping once to pick up a round paperweight and then return it to its spot. He'd finally signed the transfer papers. He was leaving Kristi.

It was high time.

He'd worked at Jensen Distributors for five years, the last two as Kristi's personal assistant. Sure he'd stayed eighteen months longer than most of her previous PAs, but he hadn't minded. Being her PA was the number-one stepping-stone in the company. Do a good job and you could almost write your own ticket.

Problem was, he'd fallen in love with Kristi a few months into being her PA. But he knew better than to try to date his boss, especially when his boss was the CEO's daughter. Dating Kristi Jensen would be career suicide. And he liked his job and the opportunities that awaited him whenever he was ready.

Which was now. She was at lunch with her boyfriend and she'd confided a few days ago that she thought Bill was ready to propose. She'd been staring at her left hand ever since.

He couldn't continue working with her this closely when there was no hope that she'd ever see him in a romantic light. So he'd cut his losses, applied for a transfer and, since Jensen moved fast, come Monday he'd be in a new job.

He stopped pacing and returned to his desk. He had put his life on hold for two years, pining for a woman he couldn't have. His parents didn't understand why he wasn't married. He was thirty-two, and in his big Catholic family that meant he was late settling down.

But how could he marry someone else when his dream girl was right in front of him? He liked everything about her: blond hair, blue eyes, dazzling smile and infectious laugh. Despite her upbringing, she wasn't pretentious. Being around her made every day a little brighter.

But even though he was transferring and she would no longer be his boss, he knew their relationship wouldn't change. He and Kristi were from different worlds. He was missing the very large personal fortune St. Louis elite like the Jensens possessed. And while Kristi might accept him, he knew her parents never would.

He logged back onto his computer, which had gone into sleep mode while he'd mulled over his future. He would tell Kristi he was transferring the moment she returned.

That resolution flew out the window when she arrived back in the office earlier than expected, her nose swollen and her eyes red and puffy. He jumped to his feet, concerned. "Are you okay?"

"Fine," Kristi managed to say, and Mitch could see where she'd smeared her makeup by wiping her eyes. She tried to put on a brave front. "What happened while I was out?"

"Not much. Everything's pretty much shut down because of the party."

"Has my dress arrived?"

The hell with protocol. Mitch stepped forward and placed a steadying hand on her forearm. "Your dress came. Barbara and Sara are already at the hotel supervising setup." Tonight's party was completely Kristi's baby. She and the entire communications department staff had been working on the company's premier event for months.

"What about the Michelson report?"

"Done, copied and sent to everyone to read before Tuesday's meeting."

"The pricing for the new brochures?"

"Waiting for the last bid spec, and I sent a reminder e-mail to Print Pro telling them they had until Monday at 9:00 a.m. or they wouldn't be considered. Everything's been done. What's wrong?"

She lifted her chin and her lips quivered. "Bill and I are through."

Mitch's heart raced. Bill was a cad of the first degree. He'd treated Kristi like an afterthought.

"I'm sorry to hear that," Mitch lied. While he'd never be able to have Kristi for himself, he wanted her to be happy. She deserved a lot better than Bill.

"If he calls or stops by, I don't want to talk to him," Kristi said. She reached into her purse, withdrew her cell phone and turned it off.

"Of course I won't let him through," Mitch said. He'd take pleasure in relaying any go-to-hell message to Bill. "Are you sure you don't want to go home early? Maybe rest up or take a nap? I can handle things here."

Kristi shook her head, and a blond strand fell out of her updo. She'd already had her hair styled for tonight's gala. "No. I'm good. Unless you can tell me how to break the news to my parents that yet again I've failed to land a husband. Thirty-five is so over the hill."

"You're not over the hill."

Her wan smile never reached her eyes. "You only think that because you're a man. Plus, you aren't turning thirty-six in a month and you don't have a biological clock ticking. Add to that parents who have wanted to be grandparents for ten years and my desire to kick Bill's ass, and tonight is not going to be fun."

"You know, if you need a date for the party, I'd be happy to take you."

Her eyes widened, and Mitch wondered how the hell those words had slipped out.

"You're sweet," Kristi finally said, cracking a grateful smile, the first real one he'd seen since she returned. "That was good for my battered pride. Thanks. But I'm sure you could do much better than me. Now, unless it's someone telling me the world's ending, I'm going to try to get some work done. Hold all my calls."

"I will." As she entered her office and shut the door, Mitch cursed fate.

DESPITE MITCH'S EARLIER reassurances otherwise, thirty-five was over the hill. As Kristi donned her red-velvet cocktail dress, the one she'd picked out especially for tonight's party, she pressed her hand against her stomach and gave one last glance over her shoulder to check her backside.

Nothing out of place. She was slim, trim and fit as someone who ran five miles a day should be.

She fingered the teardrop-diamond pendant her dad had given her on her last birthday, almost a year ago, before letting the gem fall against her chest.

Despite her resolve, she'd failed to hold back her tears on the drive back to the office. However, this necklace was the only teardrop she planned to wear tonight.

True to his word, Mitch had held all calls and the afternoon had been blissfully silent. A knock on her office door had Kristi stepping out of her private bathroom. Mitch poked his head around the door, his fingers curled over the edge. "If you don't leave now you're going to be late," he warned.

"Thanks." She waved him in, and Mitch released his grip and entered. He was the best PA she'd ever had, so she respected his opinion and knew he'd be honest. "How do I look?"

He folded his arms across his chest and studied her. She shifted nervously as the seconds ticked by. Usually Mitch had an immediate answer. After today's earlier letdown, she didn't need more bad news. "Well?" she asked, impatience getting the best of her.

"This is tricky. Would you like the politically correct answer or the one that could get me fired for sexual harassment?"

For the first time in what felt like forever, Kristi laughed. Mitch had a great sense of humor and an innate ability to put things in proper perspective. "How about the latter? I could use a pick-me-up, and as long as you don't tell me I look like an old hag, I won't fire you or tell my dad."

Mitch's lips inched upward and he winked, something she'd never seen him do. So he could flirt. Interesting.

"Well, if you weren't my boss, I'd pick you up. That's one hot dress and you look great in it. Every guy in the place will be checking you out."

She'd bought the dress hoping Bill would take notice. It had a deep V back and the front plunged enough to reveal ample cleavage without being too risqué. Perhaps to get Bill's attention she should have worn some pasties and installed a stripper's pole. She tried to push the negative thoughts aside. Anger was such a useless emotion. "Thanks."

"No problem." Mitch said, business-as-usual tone back. The Christmas party was always black tie and he tugged on the ends of his. "I never can get these tied."

"Here. Let me." Kristi moved to stand in front of him. "I sometimes think our union truck drivers have a better deal. Their celebration is beer and pork steaks in the union hall."

"Don't forget their bonus checks," Mitch added with a chuckle. She'd always liked his laugh. It was deep and low. Sensual. Yep, some woman somewhere was a fool for not snatching him up.

"Money is always a definite plus, but I was thinking more along the lines of how nice jeans sounded. Their party is much more casual."

"Yeah, but then you wouldn't be wearing that gorgeous dress."

His compliment warmed her. "Not that anyone's going to appreciate it."

"I do." His eyes met hers and the sincerity she saw there made her breath catch.

Her fingers fumbled as they undid the knot at the base of Mitch's throat. She'd stood close to Mitch on plenty of occasions, and sometimes they'd exchanged playful banter, but this was the first time she'd had butterflies in her stomach. He'd changed his aftershave to a woodsy scent and he smelled divine. Sexy.

The emotional upheaval of the breakup had to be causing her physical reaction. She downplayed his compliments. "At least someone will enjoy the dress. So you don't have a date for tonight?"

He frowned. "Was I supposed to bring one?"

"No. Of course not." It was socially acceptable if men went stag. The double standard rankled. "But you didn't ask anyone?"

"No. I broke it off with Louisa about two months ago. I didn't ask anyone else as I assumed I'd be helping set up at the hotel."

Kristi had removed him from that on-site responsibility three weeks ago. "Oh. I'm sorry things didn't work out with Louisa."

He shrugged. "It's no big deal. We weren't right for each other. I'm waiting for that one special person, no matter how long it takes."

"Yeah, if only it was that simple." She'd been dating for twenty years and had more strikeouts than she could count. At this rate she'd never get to home plate. "Then again you shouldn't have any problems locating Ms. Right."

He leaned back, ignoring his still-unknotted tie. The ends dangled, a contrast to the crisp white shirt that fit like a glove, hinting at the sculpted body beneath. "You think it'll be easy?"

"Why wouldn't it be? You have a good job. You're an attractive guy."

That was an understatement. At six foot two, and with jet-black hair and eyes the color of dark chocolate,

Mitch was hot. He was also her PA, which was why she tried not to stare at him too long.

"Women should be standing in line to date you. I mean, not me obviously since I'm your boss, but other women. I'm surprised they aren't breaking down your door."

His lips curled. "Thanks, I think."

With his Latin ancestry, Mitch's skin was a constant light tan, and his eyes were heavy lidded and soulful. His full lips framed a perfect smile.

The truth was, when she'd first met Mitch, she'd swallowed…hard. Unfortunately, her dad had definite ideas about the type of men she should date—wealthy, successful and from a good family. Larry Jensen had set the bar high. Those who didn't measure up found the door fast. With his blue-collar background, Mitch would never meet her father's standards.

Kristi shook her head, trying to rein in her wayward thoughts. "When do I need to leave?" She finished tying his bow and focused on her job and the real reason Mitch was in the room.

He checked his watch. "Three minutes ago."

The party was at an upscale hotel ballroom in Clayton, a ten-minute drive from Jensen's corporate headquarters. The only potential hitch in the evening was that St. Louis was expecting five inches of snow, but that wasn't supposed to start until well after midnight. "Then I best get going. You leaving, too?"

Mitch nodded and placed a hand on the small of her back. For some reason Kristi felt a shiver of pleasure travel down her spine. "I'll walk you out."

Chapter Two

By ten minutes to six, Kristi had lost track of Mitch, who was helping Barbara at the welcome table for tonight's event. Her team was very efficient, which meant Kristi was free to focus on her parents, who'd arrived to oversee another Jensen year-end gala.

"You did a beautiful job, dear," Kristi's mom said, surveying the full ballroom, which glittered with people dressed to the nines. The lights overhead created the perfect mood. Crystal gleamed and no expense had been spared on the rented china table settings. After dessert and a few speeches, a band would take over so that everyone could dance the night away. "You've really outdone yourself."

Kristi warmed under her mother's praise. As Emma Jensen's only child, she'd grown up knowing she was supposed to fulfill all her parents' hopes and dreams. Except for finding a husband, Kristi had met every expectation her mom and dad had set. "Thank you. I have a great staff and the hotel's new banquet manager was amazing."

"Yes, but it's all because of your leadership," her

father said. Larry Jensen was a big man, six foot six and built to match. His very presence commanded respect, and tonight was no exception.

Since her father hated feeling as if he was eating in a fishbowl, there was no head table. Her parents and three other couples would eat at a round table near the podium, and Kristi's place card was at the next table over. Bill was to have been seated to her left.

As if sensing a problem, Emma turned back to her daughter. "Where's Bill? Shouldn't he be here by now?"

The moment of truth.

"He's…" Kristi faltered as her father slid his arm around his wife's waist. A lump formed in Kristi's throat. Even though her father could be overbearing, Kristi always found herself awed by the love he had for his family and his wife.

Although she wanted a love like her parents shared, she'd been willing to settle for companionship with Bill. At her age, something was better than nothing, right?

Kristi brushed some imaginary lint from the skirt of her dress. "So where is he?" her father asked. "I'm considering buying stocks in a start-up company and I wanted to ask him about it."

Somehow she managed to speak. "He's not coming."

Her father frowned. "Why not? You invited him, didn't you? Is he out of town?"

Her shoulders slumped in defeat. "More like out of my life. He met someone else."

"Oh." Her father absorbed this. While he was adept at dealing with business crises, he wasn't good at handling Kristi's constant breakups. He simply couldn't understand what was wrong with his perfect daughter.

"Oh, honey, I'm sorry to hear that. Are you okay?" Kristi's mother gave her a sympathetic hug.

"I'll be fine," Kristi repeated the words she'd been telling herself all day as she quickly ended her mom's embrace. It was common knowledge around the firm that Kristi Jensen couldn't keep a man. Soon enough the gossip would be whispered around the watercooler that Kristi had been dumped yet again. Tonight she wanted some peace.

"I'll explain what happened when I see you on Sunday night."

"Did you invite someone else?" her father asked.

Her father—Mr. Practical. "No, he only told me the news today at lunch. Besides, I don't need a date. I'm working, remember? It's my job to make sure this party goes off without a hitch."

"That's why you have staff." The lines on Larry's forehead deepened.

"But it's still my responsibility," Kristi insisted, scanning the crowd for an escape route.

To her relief, her father leaned over and gave her a kiss on the top of the head. "Sorry. I'm being insensitive. Sometimes I forget to be a dad first. I hate seeing you hurt. Believe me, I'm already plotting Bill's demise."

"Don't go to jail on my account," Kristi said. Their

long-standing joke still made her father smile, although sadly.

"Okay, but remember, I have good lawyers. I'd get off," he finished, as was custom.

Her mother, though, continued frowning. "I still don't like you eating all alone, especially tonight. How will that look? Larry?"

Her father always deferred to his wife. He nodded. "True. The president of the union is seated at your table. We're going into contract negotiations in a few months. You need a date."

Sometimes keeping up business appearances was so archaic. Kristi opened her mouth to protest again, but a male voice spoke first. "I'll sit with her."

Kristi pivoted to see Mitch behind her. She wondered how much he'd overheard.

"I don't have a date, either, and that way there won't be any empty seats," he told her dad.

Pride had her bristling. A knight in shining armor was not required. She could handle dinner. The union president could deal.

"That would be great," her mother said with obvious relief.

"Really, there's no reason," Kristi protested, but her father's nod sealed the deal.

"That's a grand gesture, Mitch. This is perfect. I'll want to hear your impressions of the union president. Mitch's dad is a carpenter," Larry told Emma, "so his family's had a lot of experience dealing with the union."

"Dad's been in the union since he was twenty," Mitch confirmed. "Almost thirty-three years."

Kristi watched the exchange with interest. She'd known Mitch's dad was a tradesman of some sort. The fact that her dad knew Mitch's background didn't surprise her. Larry Jensen had a mind like a steel trap, which was why he and his brothers had been so successful building their business. With the issue of Kristi's dinner companion resolved, Larry guided his wife to their table.

Kristi turned to Mitch the minute her parents were out of earshot. "I didn't require a rescue."

"No, but I do." He stood so close his breath tickled her ear. "Lisa in Accounting found out I'm single. I figure eating with you is a good way to fend her off."

"Oh." She stepped back, trying to maintain a professional distance. "Then I was right. I told you this afternoon you wouldn't have any trouble finding someone new."

Mitch took a glass of wine from a passing waiter and handed it to Kristi. "Yeah, but there's only one person I'm really interested in and she's not available. I don't date for sport."

"But why not Lisa? I've met her. She's a nice girl. A little boy crazy, but sweet."

"She doesn't do anything for me."

A small chime sounded, signaling that everyone be seated for dinner. With a sweep of his arm, Mitch indicated Kristi should go first.

"So are sparks really that important?" she asked as she went by him.

Mitch's brows knit together. "There has to be something there. Something more than a pretty face and a willing body."

"Like what?"

He pulled out her chair and she sat. "I don't exactly know. When guys are young we're happy to be with any girl who pays us attention. It's hormones and physical. When we get older we get choosier. There has to be some deeper connection than sex."

She'd thought she and Bill were connected. "I guess I don't understand. Bill and I both loved Thai food, National Public Radio and walks in the park. He dumped me for a twenty-one-year-old stripper."

"Bill's an ass. Always has been."

Her mouth dropped. "Now you tell me?"

Mitch still stood above her. He shrugged. "I'm your PA. Who am I to criticize your personal life? You seemed happy."

"Blind is more like it. I have terrible guy-radar. It leads me to the wrong man every time."

Mitch settled into his chair. "You deserve to be happy."

"Yeah, we all do. Like you." Eager to get the spotlight off herself, Kristi asked, "So what about the girl you mentioned earlier, the one you said is unavailable?"

Mitch's brown eyes clouded as he focused on something over her shoulders. "Forget I mentioned that."

"Come on. Tell me. I've told you all my secrets tonight."

His tone turned wistful. "I think things could be great between us, but she has no idea how I feel. She'll never see me as anything more than a friend."

His forceful determination sounded so sure, and thank goodness she was sitting down, for Kristi's knees weakened. What would it be like to have a man who loved you that much? The only ones who'd been that enamored of Kristi had turned out to be gold diggers. She really couldn't win.

"And you can't fix that? You can't give her a clue?" Kristi's romantic notions couldn't believe a man of Mitch's caliber could fail at getting anything he wanted.

He shook his head, the ballroom lights shimmering off his black hair. "No. It's not possible. Some things aren't meant to be." Mitch's tone was flat and final, as if he'd long ago resigned himself to the situation. Their tablemates then joined them, and personal conversation ended.

Dinner was pleasant, and Mitch and Kristi made small talk with the union president and his wife and the others throughout the four courses. After dessert, Kristi excused herself and located her best friend Alison.

"Hey, what's going on? Where's Bill?" Alison asked as they made their way to the ladies' room. "Why are you eating dinner with Mitch?"

Kristi glanced around. No one was paying them any

attention. "Bill broke up with me. Mitch is my self-appointed mercy date."

Alison's horrified face was classic. She touched her friend's arm. "Oh, God. Kristi. I'm so sorry."

Kristi somehow refrained from rolling her eyes. "Tell me about it. I texted you."

"I left my phone at home by mistake and I had my work phone set to voice mail so I could get this week's employment transfers finalized. I'm so sorry I wasn't there for you."

"It's okay. I'd rather not talk about my sucky love life tonight anyway. Maybe tomorrow we could have a wine-and-cheese pity party?"

Alison nodded. "Of course. I'll send the girls to my mom's and come over. Tonight you should give yourself a night of pure unbridled lust."

"That's your answer to everything that goes wrong in my life. You know I will not go to some bar and pick up a handsome stranger."

"Yeah, I know. Although, doesn't it sound grand? Sex with no strings and no expectations. Satisfaction without heartbreak."

"We're not very good at dating, are we?" Kristi observed. While neither was the one-night-stand type, it was fun to fantasize about the possibilities.

"No. And dating the second time around is even suckier than the first. The only good part is you break up easier since you don't have as many delusions that you can somehow fix things."

"True. I didn't even protest when Bill told me he'd met someone else. I guess it gets easier."

"I've got your back."

"Thanks."

Kristi knew it was true. She and Alison had been best friends since seventh grade, and they'd attended the same college and joined the same sorority. The big difference between the two women was that Alison had gotten married at twenty-two and found herself divorced ten years later. She'd been working at Jensen Distributors ever since and raising two children as a single mom.

"So what about Mitch?" Alison asked. "He's dateless."

"Yeah. Wait, are you suggesting I go after Mitch? He works for me."

"Not anymore. He transferred. He starts a new job Monday. Didn't he tell you?"

Kristi frowned. Alison worked in Personnel. She knew all the hirings, firings and transfers. "No. He didn't."

Alison's mouth formed a little O. "Well, surely you didn't think he was staying. The company's been grooming him for something better."

"True. I'm not sure why he stayed as long as he did."

"Maybe he likes you."

Kristi remembered Mitch's mystery girl. "Highly doubtful."

"It was only a thought. Too bad you won't see much

of him anymore. You know there are people in the office I've met once and never seen again until tonight. Our building is too big and he'll be working on another floor."

The thought of not seeing Mitch bothered Kristi a lot, as did the fact that he'd transferred and not told her he was even thinking about it. "True, there are people here I've never even met."

"Your loss is someone else's gain. I wish Mitch would have transferred to Personnel." Alison pushed a tendril of brown hair away from her face. Like Kristi, she'd gotten an updo. "If something comes up and we don't see each other tomorrow, let's for sure do lunch Monday. As much as I don't want to, I should probably get back before Winston thinks I ditched him."

Kristi heard the inevitable in her friend's voice. "Are you planning on dumping him?"

"He's a good guy, but there's no excitement in our relationship. No ooh or aah. But then again, that's what got me in trouble and married."

Sparks again, or rather the lack of them, Kristi thought as she and Alison reentered the ballroom.

"Dancing's started," Alison said.

Kristi figured poor Winston's days were numbered. "You don't have to dance with him."

Alison sighed. "So you say."

As Kristi watched her walk away, she remembered how much fun they'd all had at Alison's wedding, when for one night everything had seemed perfect and it had been easy to believe in endless love.

The joyous illusion hadn't lasted. Still, Kristi knew that marriage could work—her parents were living proof.

"There you are." The warmth of Mitch's deep voice washed over her and she turned. He cut an impressive figure, so handsome in his tux. "Would you like to dance?"

The temptation of being in his arms lured her. What could dancing hurt? "Okay. One dance. Two if you're good."

"Oh, trust me, I am." His eyes twinkled.

"Oh, really? We'll see." She forced her tone to be light and casual. "By the way, I have a question for you."

"That sounds serious." He led her onto the dance floor, where he gathered her in his arms. Despite the gentleness of his touch, she tensed. "Relax," he cajoled. "I don't bite."

Which was good, because Kristi's brain had short-circuited. She knew he worked out, but the tautness of his muscles directly underneath her fingers made her stomach clench.

Give yourself a night of pure unbridled lust. Alison's words didn't seem like such a joke at the moment.

She tried to ease her grip lest she be clutching his forearms like a woman fearful for her purse. The music slowed, and he guided her even closer. Her legs brushed against his as they stepped in rhythm. "You still haven't relaxed," he chided.

How could she when she was wrapped around such a delectable man? "Trying."

His lips were dangerously close. "You're safe with me," he told her.

No, she wasn't. Dangerous, illicit thoughts ran through her mind. What would his lips on her ear and neck feel like? Would his fingers be light or heavy when they traced her skin? What did he look like naked?

Her body was on fire.

She arched back slightly so she could look up at him. The great view of his square jaw and sensual lips did little to cool her down.

Desperate, she said the only thing that could act like a bucket of cold water. "So when were you going to tell me you'd transferred?"

He sighed, his entire body releasing the breath he'd been holding. "I accepted the position before lunch. In light of Bill's news, I thought telling you today would be doubly upsetting."

"So you were going to leave me on Monday without any warning?"

"I planned to come in first thing and let you know. I'm sorry. It was bad timing and I didn't want to cause you any further pain, but it was wrong to keep this from you."

She understood his reasoning. Yet it still rankled that, like most single men in her life, Mitch had found a better offer.

"It's fine," she told him. If she repeated that mantra

enough, she might just believe it. "Everyone knows being my PA is a stepping-stone."

Kristi didn't usually wallow in self-pity, but tonight it was as if a lifetime had caught up with her. Mitch was the best PA she'd ever had. They worked so well together. She'd truly miss him.

"What will you be doing?" she asked.

"I'll be working with the Finance Department on maintaining the company's bottom-line profitability during the upcoming union contract negotiations. If I do well, they'll put me in charge of my own division."

"This sounds like the perfect opportunity for you."

Mitch's hands shifted, sending a delicious tingle across her skin, which was quite a stark contrast to the rampant melancholy overtaking her.

He sensed her mood. "I don't plan to vanish."

"It'll happen. Alison said you'd be on a different floor. You know how it gets."

"So? Let's not be strangers. I'd hate for us to lose touch. I've enjoyed working with you and consider you a good friend."

For some reason those words sounded like every other breakup speech she'd heard, even though Mitch was referring to work. She really had to get a grip.

"Mitch, don't worry about me. Enjoy what you've achieved. You've earned it."

"You're a special woman, Kristi."

But his words weren't of any comfort, for as she held him, she wished tonight could be something more. His body did something to hers—gave her sensations she'd never quite felt before. Sparks.

Wow. And with the absolute wrong guy—one her parents would never approve of. They danced a few more numbers and then Mitch guided her off the dance floor and toward the bar. "What would you like?"

She'd like what she couldn't have. What she suddenly wanted, really wanted, was for one night not to be Kristi Jensen. She wanted to be desired, to have men begging at her feet for the privilege of spending a mere second with her.

She wanted a night of passion that would leave her sated and fulfilled.

She wanted the man in front of her.

"Mitch, if I tell you something, will *you* not sue *me* for sexual harassment?"

He took a sip of the rum and Coke he'd ordered. "Why would I do that? I thought we cleared that up earlier today."

"Because what I say might make things awkward between us."

His smile reassured her. "I like to think I'm a reasonable man. I believe we're big enough people to handle whatever we need to say to each other."

"I trust you, but I'm worried this will come out wrong." She took a long sip of her own cocktail. Could she really do this? "Do you think I'm beautiful?"

He snorted in disbelief. "Remember the dress. Tonight you're the most beautiful woman here. Never doubt that."

"If I wasn't your boss, would you ask me out?"

He choked as if his drink had gone down the wrong pipe. "Kristi, Bill was a fool. It's his loss. He didn't realize how wonderful you are."

His words fed her ego and gave her much-needed confidence. "Mitch, if that's the case, can you do me one last favor? One with no strings? No expectations?"

He set his glass down. She'd never seen such intensity in his eyes, almost as if he knew what she was thinking. "What?"

"Let's leave. You and me. Take me somewhere and kiss me. I want to feel sparks."

As Mitch's mouth dropped open in surprise, Kristi stood there, refusing to look at the floor. She somehow held his gaze with her own.

She'd done it. She'd propositioned Mitch. She'd put it all out there, and to hell with the consequences. She fought the tension building in her shoulders, worked not to clench her hands. He was going to say no. Like everyone else, he'd reject her. After all, someone had to have common sense tonight.

She began to backpedal. "I shouldn't have said anything. I was out of line. Really, let's just pretend I never said any—"

"Yes."

She faltered. "Yes?"

He put a finger to her lips. "Yes."

Chapter Three

As Mitch led Kristi from the ballroom, he wondered what the hell he was doing. He'd always considered himself a man of good judgment and strong character.

Yet here he was with the last woman on earth he should be holding this tightly. Kristi Jensen was off-limits, and he'd promised to kiss her.

Once away from the ballroom, Kristi gave a soft sigh and nestled deeper into his arms. He inhaled the intoxicating scent of her hair, her perfume and her skin. There was nothing he wanted more tonight than to kiss her as much as humanly possible.

He found a secluded alcove created by oversize plants. Not as romantic as he'd like, but it would have to do. Kristi was already tugging on his jacket and raising herself on her toes. He understood. Two years was a long time to wait.

His lips found hers and a welcome shudder ran through him as he tasted her for the first time. Delicious. Her mouth was heaven and he drank in her sweetness as he deepened the kiss. Her hands wrapped around his neck and he hardened. One kiss stretched into two. Two became three. Her hands found his chest and he cupped her bottom.

She pulled back. "I have a room upstairs. Same terms."

Her eyes held hopeful expectation and he crushed his lips back to hers. He'd loved her for so long; he could deny her nothing.

She'd asked for no strings, which wasn't his style, but he wanted to make her happy. Besides, what future did they have? None. He'd even risk his own—tonight he was going to endanger his job and his future to make love to Kristi Jensen.

He planned to drown himself in those blue eyes and unpin that golden, silken hair. He'd live the fantasy— show her how a real man would treat her—before going his own way, no strings. No expectations. Like he'd promised.

As much as having a one-night stand went against his moral code, he reassured himself it would be better this way. He couldn't wait for something that never would exist, especially after tonight, no matter how much he loved her.

His feelings were best left buried.

He only had this moment. He wouldn't ruin it with silly declarations she didn't want to hear.

He jabbed the elevator button. Jensen had received some complimentary rooms from the hotel, and Kristi was staying in one of them; a few lucky employees who'd won the company's holiday raffle had the others.

When he and Kristi had arrived earlier, the bellhop had taken her overnight bag to her room.

"We don't have to do this," he said, giving her an out. The elevator doors closed behind them, providing total privacy.

She wrapped her arms around him and turned her face to his. "Yes, we do. I trust you. Prove to me I'm normal. Prove to me it's not me that's so zingless."

"It's not you." How could she ever think that? Didn't she feel what was between them? His entire body hummed.

"Ask any of my ex-boyfriends. Carl called me frigid. Mike said I talk too much. Andrew said I didn't talk enough. Clay told me I was too stuck-up, and Mark said I was too nice. Bill didn't think I was young and hot enough. I started dating at sixteen. I've had almost twenty years of losers."

Mitch realized each one had done a little number on her self-esteem and added a few more bricks to the wall surrounding her heart. He caressed her cheek with his knuckle.

"You're a beautiful and desirable woman. If I didn't work for you, I'd have asked you out years ago. And I'd have done this."

He brought his lips to hers. When she gave a soft sigh and kissed him back, he knew he was doomed.

After loving her for so long, how the hell was he supposed to leave her? He brushed aside the reasons they should stop this foolishness and instead kissed her thoroughly. They reached the eighth floor and Mitch used Kristi's key to open room 812. Except for an oversize bathroom, it was a typical hotel room: desk, two chairs and an armoire containing a TV.

Only the bed mattered.

The moment the door clicked shut behind them, he kissed her again. He tasted her sighs, and when her mouth parted slightly, he teased her lips with his tongue until she opened and let him inside.

The velvet dress cut low in the back, and a movement of his hands had him touching smooth skin, and then he pressed her closer.

He already ached, but tonight wasn't about him. It was all about her, and she needed a loving touch.

Kristi gave a soft cry and, emboldened by her response, Mitch freed one hand and sent a fingertip down her neck. He traced a straight line to where the dress made a V. Then he dipped below the fabric, found her nipple and circled it.

She trembled.

"Like that?"

"Oh, yes."

"More?" he teased.

"Uh-huh."

He smiled to himself. She was the hottest woman on

the planet and he was going to prove to her that all men weren't insensitive creeps. He freed her breast from the soft fabric and lowered his head.

As MITCH'S MOUTH found her sensitive skin, Kristi's brain registered one thing. He was already the best lover she'd ever had and they hadn't even gotten started.

She focused on the man kissing her body, making it hum like an instrument finally back in tune. He was so considerate, even folding her dress and laying it across a chair before shedding his own clothes.

Then he was with her, and Kristi was glad it was Mitch, who she knew and trusted, giving her what she'd so desperately needed

She could almost thank Bill for his foresight in dumping her and leading her to this moment.

And then Bill was forgotten—he was part of the past, and this was the present and it was beyond good.

Mitch's touch sizzled. She moaned as he teased her with his tongue, felt her body shake as his hands gripped her buttocks and drew her forward so that her hips molded to his.

He nipped gently at her lips, teasing and cajoling. He reached up and removed the pins from her hair, sending it cascading to the tops of her breasts. He lifted a strand to his lips.

And then he kissed her neck and began to work his way lower. Pleasure consumed her, and she reached for him, but Mitch brushed her hands away. "This is all for you." He brought his mouth to the juncture of her thighs.

She clutched the top of his head for support as pleasure rocked her, and then finally he joined her.

Mitch fit her perfectly, and Kristi quivered as her release began to build. He glided in and out, his body creating a timeless rhythm that brought them both to a climax where she swore she saw stars.

Then he drew her into his arms, and she rested, spent and totally fulfilled.

"Good?" he asked.

"Very," Kristi told him. He'd given her the best sex of her life. Her eyes began to close, although she wasn't tired. She was recharging for round two.

He kissed her shoulder and ran a finger down her arm.

The urge to speak overwhelmed her, but Kristi had no idea what to say. She'd never picked up anyone in her life, and this wasn't some stranger she'd climbed into bed with, but Mitch.

And he'd been incredible.

"Stop worrying," he told her.

"I wasn't," Kristi lied.

Spooned as she was, she couldn't see his face. He adjusted her hair and his breath blew warm on the back of her neck. "I know you well enough to know that you are. We said no regrets. So stop worrying. I won't tell if you don't."

Her nose wrinkled. "It seems strange that we have to worry about hiding this at our age."

"Shh." He stroked her hair. "Thinking is overrated. Just feel. It's what both of us wanted."

She registered the last part. "You wanted me?"

"Yes. A man would have to be a monk to work with you and not find you incredibly sexy."

"Really?"

"Hell, yeah. Should I tell you how often I wanted to do wicked things to you on your desk?"

He shocked her with his boldness, but she also found his speech arousing. All this time, Mitch had desired her? "Then why didn't you tell me?"

He pulled her closer. "Because I like my job and working for Jensen. And I'm not the kind of husband your dad wants for you."

"That's for sure." The words slipped out and she quickly covered her mouth. "Oops. I'm sorry."

His grip didn't change, and Kristi relaxed further as he said, "I'm not offended. I resigned myself to that fact a long time ago. Plus, you don't sleep with the boss."

"But you just did." She couldn't help herself. She giggled. "Although I'm not your boss anymore."

"Still, if your dad found out, he'd kill me."

"True. But you're already guilty."

"And willing to risk the deed again," Mitch replied, capturing both her breasts in his palms. "Tonight I exist to please you."

"Ah," she said, liking the sound of that and the re-action his touch called forth from her body.

"Can I have more of what we just did? How much stamina do you have?"

He leaned over her, and his lips curled upward in a delicious, predatory smile. He was a man's man, and until checkout time he was all hers. Shivers traveled down her spine and fresh heat pooled between her thighs.

"How many ways do you want it?" he asked, a hand sliding between her legs.

She gasped as his fingers touched her sensitive flesh. "How many ways do you know?"

"Let's find out."

As Mitch began to kiss Kristi, he made himself one last promise before all rational thought vacated his brain.

He would give her everything tonight. She'd experience a real man's touch—strong, sensual and sure. He'd make certain that when he left Kristi Jensen's bed tomorrow, he'd leave her satisfied.

The prospect of leaving her sucked, but Mitch knew this interlude with Kristi was his one, only and last.

He couldn't tell her his feelings. She'd already agreed he wasn't husband material. A physical connection would have to suffice. He'd make certain every moment was special.

Then maybe he'd finally be able to move on, find a nice girl, settle down and start a family like his mama wanted.

Although, as he slid inside Kristi's warm, waiting body, Mitch didn't know how he'd ever be able to forget her. Or pretend tonight had never happened. He'd cared for her for so long. He didn't want one night. He wanted a lifetime.

But somehow he would find the strength to walk away.

As he withdrew and then reentered, she gave a cry of pleasure. Mitch pushed all thoughts from his head. He had tonight. This moment. That had to be enough.

Chapter Four

Kristi was humming Saturday night when Alison arrived. Alison stomped the snow off her boots and shuddered as she removed her coat. "It's cold out there."

"I know. Did you have any trouble getting here?"

"No. They've got the streets cleaned."

Kristi took Alison's coat and hung it in the condo's coat closet while Alison took off her boots and placed them on the indoor mat. "They were decent this afternoon when I came home."

"Did you get sick or something? I went looking for you and you were gone."

"I went up to the hotel room for a while. Wine?"

Alison's nose wrinkled. "Ew. No, thanks. Do you have any 7UP?"

"Did you drink too much last night?" Kristi asked.

Alison turned sheepish. "Maybe. Winston was such an awful dancer it was painful. I drowned my sorrows."

"Well, lucky for you, I've got soda."

Kristi led the way into the kitchen where she poured

each of them a glass. She grabbed the bowl of popcorn she'd prepared and they both took a seat on the family-room sofa.

"This is great. Just what I needed. I even took the girls to McDonald's today because I didn't feel like cooking."

"So, is Winston history?"

"I doubt he'll want to see me again. He tried to get serious as the night went on, and the more he tried, the more I drank."

"Yuck."

"Yeah, it was bad. Mostly my fault, I admit. I fell asleep in the passenger seat of his car on the way home. Maybe I should have crashed with you since Bill was a no-show."

"Uh, that wouldn't have worked."

Alison arched a brow. "Why not? You were alone, weren't you?"

"I, um...." Kristi paused as a blush stole across her face.

"What did you do? Better yet, *who* did you do?"

Kristi pressed her lips together, but she couldn't contain herself. "Mitch."

"You picked up Mitch!"

"Yeah." A warm fuzzy feeling stole over Kristi and she sat there dreamily until Alison waved a hand in front of her face.

"You have got to explain all of this to me. Every-thing."

When Kristi finished, Alison leaned back, stunned. "I wouldn't have thought you had it in you."

"Me neither. But I wanted sparks and, man, there were plenty."

"Wow. Mitch. I should have seen that coming."

Kristi nibbled on a handful of popcorn. "He left before checkout. We had a room-service brunch. It was sweet."

"Sounds like it. I'm jealous. I woke up to two fighting kids and a massive headache. So, will you see him again?"

"No. It was one night. We both agreed to that."

"You're also consenting adults. You can change your mind."

Kristi sighed. "One small problem with that idea. My dad."

"Yeah, he can be difficult."

"The understatement of the year. You know we always have a family dinner on Sunday night. My mom called me earlier and they've invited some friends to join us. They're bringing their son Brock."

Alison cringed and gave a low whistle. "They aren't wasting any time, are they? Let the matchmaking begin."

"Yippee. I'm sure if I don't hit it off with Brock they'll find someone else."

For a minute, the only sound was crunching as they contemplated the situation over popcorn.

"So the sex was really good, huh?" Alison asked.

Kristi nodded. "The best. I have absolutely no regrets."

Seven weeks later

"You have to be kidding me." Kristi's mouth dropped open and she gaped at her doctor. "You're going to have to repeat that. I'm sure I misunderstood."

"I said you're pregnant."

Okay, she had heard him correctly the first time. Dr. Joftus, the internist who she'd been seeing since she was twenty years old, stood there awkwardly. "Not stomach flu. Not indigestion. Pregnant."

Kristi shook her head. "Not possible. I'm on the pill. I made an appointment because I kept throwing up."

Dr. Joftus looked sympathetic. "The tests we ran clearly show you're pregnant. I suggest you make an appointment with your ob-gyn so he can do an ultrasound or blood work. There's no question with those."

"I will." Kristi left his office. When she'd made the appointment with Dr. Joftus, she'd figured she'd leave with some medicine for her constant upset stomach, not a nine-month diagnosis of unwed motherhood.

It was the beginning of February, and she'd entered the twilight zone.

Worse, her ob-gyn, who managed to work her in later that same afternoon, confirmed Dr. Joftus's diagnosis. The ultrasound was proof positive.

"See that little grain of rice?" Dr. Krasnoff pointed to an image on the screen. "That's your baby."

Any excitement over her impending motherhood bypassed Kristi as she watched the tiny sliver on the screen. Instead of joy, panic set in.

She'd turned thirty-six a week ago and she'd been a bit under the weather. Never would she have expected this. But there in black-and-white was proof.

"I still don't understand how this is possible. I was on the pill."

"There's always the chance that birth control will fail. Only abstinence is a hundred percent effective. Maybe you didn't take a pill or two at the exact time of day. You are on a very low dose, so it's important to be consistent. Were you taking any antibiotics?"

She'd had a sinus infection a week before the Christmas party and Dr. Joftus had given her a prescription. "I was. But I've never had an issue before."

"They can make the pill less effective, and it only takes one sperm to fertilize. Should we talk options?"

Kristi chewed her bottom lip. "There are no options."

Dr. Krasnoff removed the wand from Kristi's belly and waited.

Kristi jutted her chin forward. "I'm keeping it. I never would consider doing anything else, even if I'm going at it alone. Hello, single motherhood."

Dr. Krasnoff wiped off the gel. "I take it the father isn't involved."

Therein lay the problem. "I haven't seen him. Not since the fateful night."

Mitch had started his new job on Monday, and on Tuesday, Kristi's new PA, Molly, had taken over his old desk.

Considering she'd said "no strings," she'd been

grateful for how large Jensen was, and that Mitch had kept his word not to contact her. She'd had no reason to contact him. While she might long for another night with Mitch, one had been her limit. She hadn't expected this complication.

"Your next appointment is in a month unless there are problems," Dr. Krasnoff said as she handed Kristi a prescription for prenatal vitamins. "Make the appointment on your way out and I'll see you then."

The rest of the day followed in a daze, until Kristi found herself at Alison's later that night. She'd debated canceling their dinner plans, but hadn't had the heart or a good enough excuse to call off the date they'd had planned for several weeks.

"And here I was afraid you were going to back out on me again," Alison joked as she opened the door to her Glendale bungalow.

"I've been under the weather," Kristi said, stepping inside and taking off her coat.

"It'll get better. According to the groundhog yesterday, winter's over." Two girls, one five and one seven, skidded to a stop in the foyer.

"Hey, Aunt Kristi," they chorused, before taking off once more after the cat, who'd stopped long enough for the girls to catch up.

"They plan on brushing Fluffy," Alison said. "The cat has to make a game of it first. He's an old softie."

"Exercise for all of them," Kristi remarked as she followed Alison into the kitchen. A pot of stew bubbled on the stove.

"Wine?" Alison asked.

"No. Water's fine."

Alison's eyebrow rose. "Since when do you turn down a glass of wine? Are you that ill?"

"I don't feel like drinking tonight." Kristi dropped her coat over the back of a chair and plopped down. She stretched out her feet as Alison handed her a glass of ice water.

"You aren't contagious, are you?"

Kristi shook her head and swallowed the hysterical laughter that threatened to bubble forth. Pregnancy was an emotional roller coaster. No wonder she'd been so moody lately. "No, I saw the doctor. It's nothing you or the girls can catch."

As Alison turned to uncork the wine, the youngest, Carly, bounded into the kitchen. "Mom, Kelsey won't let me brush Fluffy."

Alison wiped her hands on her apron, walked to the door and yelled, "Kelsey, let Carly have a turn. Don't make me come in there."

"Is that effective?" Kristi asked as Alison returned.

Alison poured herself a glass of merlot. "I have no clue. There are days I question everything and think I'm the world's worst mother." She raised her glass. "Sure you don't want any of this? It's pretty good stuff."

"I'm sure," Kristi replied.

"Well, more for me."

Alison sipped her wine and Kristi's mouth watered. Since she hadn't planned on being pregnant, she hadn't even considered there were things she wouldn't be able to eat, drink or do. The amount of upcoming changes was quickly becoming overwhelming.

"So, how was that last guy you went out with?" Alison asked.

"Fine." Kristi hadn't thought about James since their date a week ago. He'd been a blind date arranged by her dad.

Alison folded her arms and waited.

Kristi sighed, knowing she really couldn't hide anything from her friend. "Okay, he was boring. We went to the symphony with my parents. He's a nice guy, but dull as dishwater."

"He's not Mitch," Alison filled in.

"No one's Mitch," Kristi admitted.

"At least you had one great night with Mitch."

"Which is what I wanted. Nothing more," Kristi replied quickly, wishing she had more than water in her glass. She didn't need to think of Mitch, or his role in helping her get to this blessed state. Despite her condition, the sparks had been far too nice to regret.

Alison moved to the stove, opened the lid on the stockpot and stirred. "This is ready." She went to the door and called for the girls.

"What can I do to help?" Kristi asked.

"Nothing, you're company. Sit there and relax."

"Yes, ma'am," Kristi replied, taking a sip of water. Her stomach growled and she hoped that was a positive sign. She hadn't been able to keep down much food.

Soon all four had said grace and Alison spooned out stew while Kelsey passed around bread and salad.

Kristi's nose wrinkled. The lettuce was covered with ranch dressing, making the salad appear white and slimy. Kristi's taste buds soured.

Normally she loved salad with ranch. She returned the bowl to the center of the table without taking any.

"No salad, either?" Alison asked, her eyebrows knitting together.

"No. I'm not very hungry tonight." Kristi lifted her fork and sampled the stew on her plate. "This is delicious, though."

"Thanks. It's my specialty. The secret is using one of those sauce packets you find in the soup aisle."

"I'll have to remember to try that."

"Yeah. Like you ever turn on the stove," Alison snorted. "Can you even boil water?"

Kristi speared a piece of meat. "Yes. You put it in the microwave for five minutes."

"I can make spaghetti," Kelsey announced.

"Yes, you can," Alison acknowledged.

"That's great," Kristi said. She'd had dinner at Alison's often, even when the girls were babies. She'd been the third person to hold Kelsey. By September she'd have her own child. The thought boggled her mind.

Just like Alison had to put the girls first, Kristi now had to think of her baby. She unconsciously dropped a hand into her lap and touched her belly. She'd had only a few hours to let the news that she was pregnant sink in.

"Guess what, Aunt Kristi? I helped make dessert. It's

brownies," Carly boasted, and Kristi shook herself and focused.

She'd been zoning out a lot more lately. Years ago when Alison had been pregnant, she'd been so flighty that she'd sworn babies ate brain cells. Did that happen this early? Kristi resolved to get one of those what-to-expect books.

"Are you sure you're feeling okay?" Alison had stopped eating and was staring at Kristi oddly.

"I'm fine." Her stomach grumbled, although this time not in a good way.

"You sure? You're turning a little green and I haven't poisoned anyone with bad cooking in years."

Kristi's stomach rumbled, and she pressed her napkin to her lips.

"Are you sick, Aunt Kristi?" Carly asked.

Kristi stood. "No, sweetie. I'm going to use the bathroom, that's all."

"That way," Kelsey directed helpfully, although Kristi knew exactly where the commode was.

Five minutes later, she heard a knock on the door. The handle rattled as Alison checked if the door was locked. "You aren't okay, so what's up? I'm coming in."

"I'm fine," Kristi tried, but Alison entered anyway.

Alison crossed her arms, as she saw Kristi sitting on the floor. "I hate it when you try to lie to me. And I'm pretty sure the bite of stew you ate didn't do this to you."

"No, it wasn't that."

"I didn't think so. Let me guess. If you saw the doctor today and you're not contagious, then you have only one other excuse. I know all the signs. I've been there myself. Twice. You're pregnant, aren't you?"

"Is it that obvious?"

"I've got five older sisters. There's no symptom I haven't either had myself or seen one of them get. The first trimester is the hardest."

"This hasn't been fun," Kristi agreed. "I thought I had stomach flu. I didn't even realize the truth."

Believing her stomach to be empty and settled, Kristi rose to her feet and washed her hands. Alison tossed her a towel. "So whose is it? And does he know?"

"You mean, you have to ask?"

"Well, you did rebound to Mitch the day Bill dumped you."

"It's not Bill's. I had a period after we last slept together."

Alison clasped her hands together. "Thank God. You don't need to be tied to that loser for the rest of your life."

"I don't want to be tied to Mitch, either."

"Are you going to tell him?"

"I found out today. I haven't even had time to think about this. I'm still rather stunned." She tossed the cup into the trash can and followed Alison into the kitchen. The girls had finished eating, so they had the table to themselves.

"What if Mitch doesn't want to be a dad?" Alison

asked. "I don't think you should tell him. He'll feel guilty and insist on doing the right thing."

"Mitch wouldn't push me into marriage," Kristi defended.

Alison fingered her wineglass. "Yeah, but can you risk it? You're going to have enough problems on your hands dealing with your father. If he finds out the baby is Mitch's, he'll fire Mitch in a second. And can you picture your dad's face? Mitch is an employee. He is *not* what your country-club parents want for a son-in-law. They aren't going to be happy anyway knowing you're knocked up."

Kristi contemplated that. "What a mess."

"You know I'm here for you." Alison said.

Kristi nodded. Alison was someone she could count on. "I do and thanks. Although, don't tell anyone. I need time to figure out what I'm going to do."

Alison feigned indignation. "Who do you think I am? I'm not a gossip girl."

Kristi frowned as she suddenly thought of something. "It's going to be bad when my pregnancy becomes gossip at the country club. I can survive that. I'm not sure about my parents."

Alison patted her hand. "Your parents are tough. Your dad runs one of the most successful businesses in the city. The gossip won't last long—they're too afraid of him."

"Everyone will ask who the father is."

"Say you don't know. Your parents have thrown so

many guys at you they have to think you slept with some of them."

Kristi shuddered. "These are my parents. And if I say I don't know, I'll look like a tramp. I can't tell them it is Mitch's. As you said, my dad would fire him. I promised him no strings, and a baby is one big string."

"So don't tell him or your parents. Make things easy and protect yourself from any entanglements. Tell people you went to a sperm bank or something."

"We'll see," Kristi said. "We'll see."

Chapter Five

Two weeks later Kristi shut the door behind her mother's latest blind-date fix-up and turned the dead bolt of her parents' front door. She'd survived the latest dinner party and matchmaking attempt.

Not that Bryan wasn't a great guy. He certainly fit all the social requirements—he was charming, well connected and had a high-profile career as an up-and-coming criminal attorney. He had sharp blue eyes and dressed impeccably, and he was pretty good-looking.

But there had been no sparks. Nada. Zilch. Zip. It had all been rather depressing.

"So, Bryan's sweet, isn't he?" her mother said, coming into the foyer with a glass of brandy.

"We need to talk," Kristi said as she followed her mother into the library where her dad sat in a wingback chair, brandy also in hand.

Never one to mince words, her father asked, "So, what did you think of Bryan?"

"He's nice," Kristi hedged. She took a seat next to the fire.

"He liked you," her mom said.

Kristi exhaled. She hated to disappoint her parents, but knew she couldn't put off her announcement any longer. Time for the moment of truth. "It's not going to work."

Her mother's forehead creased. "Why ever not? He's a wonderful young man. He's your age."

"He's been concentrating on climbing the corporate ladder, so he hasn't dated much. He made full partner this year. He's got lots of potential," her dad added.

Kristi folded her hands in her lap. She took a deep breath. "I don't want to be fixed up anymore."

Both her parents frowned, distressed. "We thought you wanted our help."

"You're not getting any younger," her dad added. "How will you ever find a husband?"

Kristi winced and gritted her teeth. "I'm well aware of my age."

Her father scowled. "So what's the problem?"

"Don't you want to get married?" Her mother's soft-spoken question revealed she was heartbroken by the idea.

"Yes, I do, but I have other things on my mind. It's not a good time, anyway."

She could see her dad bite back another age-related comment.

Emma leaned forward. "I know Bill broke your heart, but you can't let one bad apple spoil the bunch. It's been months."

"I am moving forward. I've decided, though, that I

don't want to put my life on hold. I've decided to have a baby."

Her father sputtered his brandy. "You're not married."

She'd debated for days how to best approach telling them. "Dad, women don't need to be married in order to have children."

"They do in my house."

"I don't live here. I've been on my own for fifteen years."

"Well," her dad harrumphed.

"I'm sure you've thought about this, but really, a child needs two parents." Her mother tried to soothe the growing tension.

"It's a little late to worry about that," Kristi said.

"Meaning?" Her father didn't miss a thing.

"Congratulations. Mom, Dad, you're going to be grandparents."

If she'd been expecting squeals of delight, she'd have been disappointed. Instead, her mother and father froze and stared, mouths agape. Her father recovered first. "You don't look pregnant."

"I am. I've already seen the doctor. I'm due in September."

This caught her father off guard. "How did this happen?"

"The usual way," Kristi replied, wincing at their exchange of distressed looks.

Her mother smiled weakly. "Well, Larry, we've always wanted to be grandparents."

"Not this way," her father growled.

"It's not like I'm sixteen and in high school. There's no social stigma."

"Of course there is. You aren't married."

"Yes, but as you pointed out, I'm not getting any younger. Why shouldn't a woman of my financial means have a baby? I can well afford it. Celebrities do it all the time."

"You aren't one of those flighty actresses. You're a Jensen, damn it," her dad retorted.

Her mother wrung her hands. "Please. Let's not argue tonight. It's not what we wanted, but it's happening whether we like it or not. A little bundle of joy. I'll be a grandmother."

She was beginning to appear much happier; however, Kristi's dad's mood had soured further. "Is the father involved? Who is he?"

"No, he's not involved. He doesn't know and I want to leave him out of this."

Her father's scowl deepened. "I can make him pay. I can make him marry you."

"Which is exactly what I don't want," Kristi insisted, clenching her fists. "Let's concentrate on being happy."

"I'm worried you haven't thought this through," her father said. "How are you going to work? You have a job, you know."

"There are millions of women who balance work and motherhood just fine."

"You're an executive. You aren't like most other working moms," her dad pointed out.

"Which means I can afford a nanny and all the help I need."

"I would never have wanted help from a nanny. A child needs a full-time mother," Emma inserted.

"You'll take a leave of absence," her father decided.

Kristi exhaled sharply, blowing a wayward strand of hair off her face. "As much as I know you want to help, the choices are mine to make."

"Well, you don't seem to be making the best choices these days," her father retorted.

"Larry!" her mother admonished.

"Sorry," he mumbled, but Kristi could tell that it was only a matter of time before he'd return to the topic.

"Dad," Kristi began, determined to salvage something of the conversation. "I know I've disappointed you. I'll admit, this was accidental. But it's a good kind of accident. And I'm in control of the entire situation."

"Now," her father muttered.

She ignored him. "You'll have to trust me. I can handle being pregnant and doing my job. I will not fail at either."

"Of course you won't," Emma said. Larry tapped his fingers on the brocade chair arm.

The silence lengthened and Kristi squirmed. "It'll be fine."

Her father didn't look convinced. "We'll see, won't we?"

"OUCH. I'M SORRY it didn't go well," Alison said Monday over lunch.

Kristi nodded. "They weren't pleased. My dad even said that Bryan probably wouldn't mind a ready-made family. I told him that while I like to read romance novels, my life isn't one."

"Ouch."

"I apologized. I still feel bad. He meant well."

"I don't think so."

Kristi frowned. "What's going on?"

"Your cousin Brett's been moved to your department starting Wednesday."

"You're kidding," Kristi said. At twenty-seven, Brett was the youngest of Kristi's uncle Marvin's kids and if he was being moved into Communications, the writing was on the wall. He was being groomed to replace her. She'd committed the mortal sin of failing to marry before getting pregnant.

"Great. This is just fabulous news. Now what am I going to do?"

"I have no idea."

Kristi pushed her lunch plate aside. She'd lost what little appetite she had. "You did the right thing. Thanks for telling me. At least I won't be blindsided."

Kristi was still contemplating her newest dilemma when she walked out of her office a few hours later, a file folder tucked under her arm. She glanced around. Her staff was hard at work. Molly rose. "Do you need me to take that somewhere for you?"

Kristi shook her head. She'd been sitting most of the day. "No, I'll do it. I need the walk."

At her first monthly visit, Dr. Krasnoff had advised Kristi to take a five-minute stroll every few hours if possible, so the folder was a good excuse to leave her office and stretch her legs. She bypassed the elevator, opting for the stairs.

She went down three flights, surprising a few employees near the copy room when she emerged. Kristi never visited this floor; the employees here managed distribution, truck routes and retail store accounts.

She found Adam's office and spoke with him for a few minutes about the free rally-towel promotion. The towels would be handed out at an upcoming St. Louis Blues home game and there would be store displays accompanying the promotion two weeks prior.

Then it was back to the stairwell for the hike upstairs. She hadn't made it one floor when the door above her opened and footsteps sounded. Whoever was descending was in a hurry. Kristi paused on the landing, figuring she'd let the person pass by.

The metal stairs clanged as a suit-covered figure flew down. She'd recognize that physique anywhere. Mitch.

Seeing her, he skidded to an abrupt halt. "Hey."

"Hi." She swallowed and tried to catch her breath. He'd recently had his hair cut—the dark locks were shorn short and straight. Before he visited the barbershop, the ends would curl at the nape of his neck and his hair would become wavy. He looked fantastic, and her fingers itched to touch his clean-shaven jaw.

"How are you?" he asked.

"I'm fine." She remained still, refusing to squirm as his eyes inspected her from head to toe.

"Have you lost weight?"

With all the morning sickness and an unsettled stomach keeping her from eating, Kristi had lost five pounds. Dr. Krasnoff had told her not to worry, that she'd gain the weight back once the first trimester was over. "A little. Not too much."

"You haven't been sick, have you?"

She heard concern in his voice, and a sense of longing shot through her. She missed Mitch and the way he always noticed the little things. "No. I'm fine."

"Fine. You know what that means?"

"Frightened, insecure, neurotic and emotional." He'd told her that definition once.

The corners of his lips inched upward as she remembered. "So?"

"I really am fine, and none of those."

He chuckled at that. "So how is life treating you? Not having more guy trouble, are you?"

"I've given up dating. It's a belated New Year's resolution and I've even shared it with my parents." She stood there awkwardly and changed the subject. "So you like your new job?"

"Love it," Mitch said. He wiped the wide smile away. "Sorry. I mean, I liked working for you."

"It's all good. I understand. I'm glad you enjoy what you're doing."

Mitch had obviously moved on and settled in. She resisted the sudden urge to ask if he'd been able to land the girl of his dreams. "Well, it was good seeing you. I should get back upstairs. I have work to do."

She kept her tone neutral. No need for Mitch to sense that something was wrong, either personally or workwise. Running into him like this was hard enough. She couldn't help remembering their last moments together and the way his lips had felt on hers, the way his scent had lingered on her skin long after their love-making.

She attempted to pass Mitch and head to her floor, but he placed a hand on her arm. Her skin tingled.

"It's good to see you. I've been thinking a lot about you. Wondered how you were," he said. The intensity in his gaze unnerved her and she forced a light laugh.

"Same old, same old. The Communications Department is boring."

"I don't care about that. Are you doing okay?"

She lifted her shoulders in a shrug. "Why wouldn't I be?"

He removed his hand and coolness fell. While safer, she missed his touch.

He shook his head. "Never mind. I shouldn't have pried. It's just that I'm not a one-night-stand type of guy. It's never been my style. I need you to know that."

"I do."

"Then I guess I shouldn't have worried."

Mitch had to be the sweetest man she'd ever met. He deserved not to have coals heaped on his head by her father. She had to protect him from the truth. "You did what I asked you to do. We hooked up, nothing more. I'm sorry if you worried, but I've been fine."

Mitch looked as if he'd been ready to say something, but had changed his mind. "If you're okay then."

"Never better," Kristi said, managing to keep from touching her stomach as she did twenty times a day. She should tell him. He'd hear soon enough. She had no more than two months before she'd begin to show.

But Mitch didn't need to suffer her father's wrath. He had a bright future ahead, and maybe a chance to find true love. She'd gotten herself into this mess. She'd handle it alone.

Mitch took a step toward the stairs. "Well, I'm late for a meeting. You take care of yourself."

"I will." Kristi watched as he continued down the stairs and out of sight.

Seeing him had been a surprise, but she'd survived. They'd only had sex, so the sense of loss she was feeling had to be hormonal. She shushed the part of her conscience that urged her to go after him, and clung to her decision to keep her secret.

Mitch and she had shared a moment. Nothing more. She had enough to worry about with Brett's arrival into her department, and the doctor had told her to reduce her stress level. Mitch had moved on, and she knew what her already unhappy father would do should her baby's parentage be exposed. Mitch would not survive the meltdown.

Chapter Six

Mitch had been five minutes late to his meeting, but luckily Marvin Jensen had been delayed, as well. Unsettled from bumping into Kristi, Mitch found it difficult to concentrate on what was being discussed.

Despite her adamant reassurances otherwise, Kristi hadn't been her normal, robust self. Her cheeks were a tad hollow and she was very pale. He couldn't help wondering if she was really as healthy as she claimed.

He should have checked in on her sooner, but he was having a hard enough time honoring her wish to leave things at one night. He'd known that seeing her would only make it more difficult. Plus his new job had him working more hours a week than he had being Kristi's PA, and his job with her had been intense.

He was currently supervising the financial analysis for the union negotiations. He had numbers for everything—health care costs, salary increase percentages and retirement benefits.

Negotiations required examining every bottom line with microscopic precision. After several years of layoffs in the St. Louis area at other companies of similar size, both the union and management were understandably wary of ceding too much. The first meeting between the two sides was scheduled for next week.

Mitch was still mentally crunching numbers later that night at his parents' house. They'd gathered for his father's birthday, and Mitch's mother was in the kitchen with his sisters. The entire family was present—including his sister Maria's husband, Paul, and sister Lauri's boyfriend of the past year, Cristos.

Except for Mitch, who'd just come upstairs, all the men were in the basement, playing pool. Maria handed him his niece. "Here. Take your goddaughter and get your mind off whatever's troubling you."

Six-month-old Jane made a razzing sound as Mitch took her. With dark hair and full lips, she was a mini-version of her mom. Mitch dropped a kiss on Jane's forehead. She smelled like baby powder.

"You are such a cute thing," Mitch told her. "Wanna fly?" She giggled as he flew her around the living room like an airplane.

"So what's got you all hot and bothered anyway?" Maria asked. Toting Jane, Mitch followed Maria into the dining room, where she began to set the table.

"Work. That's it."

"Liar." She handed Jane a teaspoon, and her daughter squealed before immediately putting the shiny object in her mouth. Mitch reached for an extra napkin, getting ready for the utensil's drool-covered removal.

"I'm not lying," he replied, catching Jane as she made a dive for another spoon. "I had an intense afternoon meeting. You'd be amazed at how much detail goes into contract negotiations. Behave," he told Jane as she leaned forward again.

She grinned, showing off the two top teeth that had recently cut through. Mitch couldn't help himself. He smiled back. He'd been sixteen when his youngest sister, Amy, had been born, and with plenty of siblings in between, he was well versed in baby antics. To divert her, he held Jane high and flew her around the table again.

"Sometimes I think she likes you better than her dad," Maria said. "He treats her as if she's fragile."

Paul was an accountant in a major firm—a pure numbers guy and paper pusher. His job allowed Maria to stay home with the kids, and Mitch respected that. For a moment he wondered if Kristi would be the type to stay home and raise children.

Nah. Mitch couldn't picture that. Her father had made her work hard for Jensen's number-five spot. The position hadn't been handed to her and she wouldn't give it up easily.

"You have that faraway look on your face. Don't tell me you're thinking of *her.*"

"Who?" Mitch hedged. He hadn't realized Maria could read him so well. His sister's lips puckered in solid disapproval.

"You know who. The one you've pined over for years. The one who made this year's Christmas party so extra special."

"I never should have told you what happened," Mitch snapped. Jane, sensing his mood, stilled.

Mitch worked to release the building tension. Not quite a year apart in age, he and Maria had always been confidants. Yet it had been a week before he'd allowed Maria to pry the secret of that night from him. She'd caught him in a vulnerable moment, when Mitch had been replaying everything in his head and wishing things could have turned out differently. Holding Kristi in his arms and then walking away from her the next morning had been torture.

"It's always good to talk to someone and you were moping around," Maria said.

"I wasn't."

Maria's arched eyebrow told him she knew this time he was clearly lying, and, table finished, she reached for Jane, who held tightly on to her spoon and her uncle's neck.

"Mitch, you have to stop the daydreaming and wishful thinking. You got what you wanted. You had one night with her, which was more than you ever expected. Now move on," Maria advised.

"I saw her today." Mitch peeled Jane off, and she went willingly when she saw her mom held out another shiny spoon. "Something's wrong with her. She didn't look well."

Maria settled Jane on her hip. "Mitch, you can't live your entire life worrying about Kristi Jensen. She's a big girl and she has her own family."

"Yeah, but—"

"Why is Mitch worried about his boss?" Lauri interrupted, entering with a steaming bowl of green beans in her hands.

"I'm not worried," he protested. No one else in his family needed to know his business. Maria's involvement was bad enough.

"You are worrying," Maria repeated, looking at Lauri for moral support. "And she's no longer his boss."

"I had a crush on my boss once," Lauri said.

"You were twenty then and nothing happened," Maria reminded her twenty-seven-year-old sister. "And that's not what Mitch and I were discussing."

"What am I missing?" This from twenty-five-year-old Kathryn, who entered with a platter of sliced ham. Mitch rolled his eyes heavenward.

"Something about Mitch's boss," Lauri replied, starting back to the kitchen.

"So I missed something?" Kathryn set the ham down and looked first at Maria then Mitch.

"No. It's nothing." Mitch shot Maria a warning glance and then hightailed it to the basement. If food was ready and going onto the table, it was time to get the guys.

The dining-room table only sat eight, and as there were ten immediate family members, one husband and one guest, a card table had been placed at the end, where it jutted out into the living room as it had for years at family celebrations. Having eaten earlier, Jane amused herself with toys in a playpen located near her mom.

"So I have news," Lauri said once dinner wound

down. She'd waited until her father had opened all his birthday presents and was on his second helping of cake and ice cream. She reached over and squeezed Cristos's hand as all heads swiveled expectantly.

"And what's the news?" her father asked.

Next to Mitch, his sister took a deep breath. "Cristos asked me to marry him and I've said yes."

"With your permission, sir," Cristos added.

The room felt silent, as Michael Robbins looked first at his daughter, then at the man holding her hand, and then back to his daughter. He nodded. "Yes."

Bedlam erupted as Mitch's mom jumped to her feet and everyone, including Mitch, rose to hug Lauri or pat Cristos on the back. Lauri put on her ring, and Mitch, a bit overwhelmed with the craziness of the moment, cleared some dishes.

"Escaping?" Maria asked, entering with some dirty plates of her own.

"You are annoying today," Mitch told her. He knew exactly why his sister had followed him.

"Well, look on the bright side. Her wedding gets the pressure off you. Mom's got someone else to focus on. The order's been jumped. You don't have to get married next. You're free."

"That's a bit cynical," Mitch replied.

"Everyone knows Mom wants you to settle down." Maria loaded some of the serving platters into the dishwasher.

"Thirty-two isn't that old. I have years left. It's not like I can't find someone when the time's right."

"The timing's never going to be right as long as you continue to hold out for Kristi. She's keeping you from finding someone nice."

"I know," Mitch said.

"So do something about it. Get back on the scene. I met a nice single mom at the YMCA playgroup."

"No." Mitch's retort was sharp and quick.

Maria tilted her head and drew back. "So much for getting over Kristi."

"It's not that. I don't need anyone's help. I can find my own dates," he insisted.

"What's wrong with a nudge? She's a sweetheart and pretty. What would it hurt to meet her? Join Paul and me for some drinks after work."

"No," Mitch repeated, but more gently this time.

"Mitch..." Maria began before their mother bustled in and grabbed a clean dishrag so she could dab her wet eyes.

"Isn't it wonderful?" she asked. "He's so perfect for her."

"He is," Maria replied, giving her mom a hug.

"Mitch, now if we could only find you someone." His mother looked at him hopefully.

Maria shot him a pointed glance and Mitch mentally counted to ten.

"I liked that last girl you dated. What was wrong with her? Louisa, wasn't it?" his mother asked.

"We weren't compatible."

"Shame," she said. Then she brightened. "Lauri

never said if they'd picked a date. Perhaps in the summer since they're both teachers."

With that, she made a beeline for the dining room.

"We all liked Louisa," Maria pointed out.

"She was nice," Mitch admitted.

"But she's not Kristi Jensen."

"No one is." He thought for a minute. Louisa had been almost complacent. She'd make the perfect, dutiful, boring wife. Kristi was dramatic. Ambitious. The room came to life with her in it. He'd hated hurting Louisa, but he couldn't lead her on. The idea of waking up next to her for the next fifty years had been terrifying.

"Until you let Kristi go, no one will reach the pedestal you've put her on," Maria advised.

She was right. The idea of being with anyone else held little appeal. Making love to Kristi had ruined him.

As Mitch's father entered the kitchen, Maria slid out. His dad reached into the refrigerator and got a beer. He offered one to Mitch, who shook his head.

"Okay then. Suit yourself." His father leaned back against the counter. "Your mom's already going nuts in there."

"You knew she would."

His dad took a long sip. "Yep."

"You know I'll help out financially."

His dad nodded. "I know you will, whether I agree with it or not. But you really have done enough already."

Mitch shrugged. "What else am I going to spend my money on? I've got enough saved and my house is almost paid off. Let me help make Lauri's wedding special."

Mitch might not be part of the elite circle the Jensens socialized with, but he was good with money. When his dad had lost his job a year earlier, Mitch had started covering some of his parents' expenses. Eight kids meant a lot of bills, and now a lot of college tuition.

"I'll let you know," his dad said.

Mitch's dad had a great deal of pride. "Families have to stick together. You know I've already set up a savings account for Jane."

"You're a good man, son," his father said. "You still liking your new job?"

"I love it."

"Just be sure you do everything to keep it. In this economy you never know what'll happen."

"I'll do that," Mitch promised. With his family counting on him, he had more than himself to think about.

TIME SLID BY QUICKLY, and negotiations began and immediately intensified. March had roared in like a lion, and neither side had conceded anything. As the end of March approached, very little had been accomplished, but as negotiations were still ongoing, that was considered a positive sign. The contract didn't expire until April 30.

"Good job," Marvin Jensen told him once the union

leaders left the second-floor conference room after the day's meeting. "You were really sharp today."

"Thanks," Mitch replied.

Marvin was Larry's younger brother and third in command, and he was overseeing the new contract. Marvin gestured toward the three other men who also comprised the negotiations team. "We're going to Findlay's for a round of cocktails. Care to join us?"

It was a surprising offer to hang out with the top brass, and after working with them this closely for over a month, Mitch knew better than to refuse. "I'd be honored."

Marvin glanced at his watch. "Great. Meet us there in an hour. Tell the hostess to show you to my table."

"Thank you." Mitch picked up his briefcase and followed the other men out.

After returning to his office to file a report, Mitch left for the restaurant, arriving at Findlay's promptly on the hour. Marvin and the other men were already seated, and Mitch was surprised to see that Kristi's father had joined them.

Mitch had been invited to drinks with the inner circle.

"Mitch." Larry Jensen shook Mitch's hand in greeting. "Glad you could make it."

Me, too, Mitch thought as he took the last open chair.

As the night continued, he couldn't believe his luck, or how well he'd fit in. The evening began to wind down and Mitch made a motion to go, but Larry pressed him to stay and keep him company for dinner.

"You're a young, single guy. Got anywhere else to be?" Larry asked.

"Uh, not tonight," Mitch had admitted.

"Then it's settled. Emma's at her bridge group and the house is far too empty when she's gone. Marvin's got to run, so let me buy you a meal. Marvin tells me you've been doing a great job and have had some valuable insights. I'd like to hear more about them."

It wasn't until they were drinking after-dinner coffee that Larry said, "Mitch, I've got to tell you I'm impressed with your savvy. You should have transferred a long time ago. However, I can understand why you didn't. Kristi's quite the prize, isn't she?"

Mitch waited expectantly, his fingers poised on the handle of his coffee cup. He had no idea how to answer that, and assumed the question was rhetorical as Larry leaned back and settled himself deeper into the plush wingback chair. Findlay's had the old-world air of a private club.

"Mitch, I've got a small problem I'm hoping you can help me with. I trust your discretion and would like this to stay between us."

Mitch nodded.

"You worked with Kristi for two years. During that time, did she ever strike you as depressed or anxious?"

He'd been correct. Something had been off with Kristi when he'd last seen her. "No. She was upset over

Bill, but no more so than with any other breakup I saw her go through. Is something wrong?"

Larry Jensen exhaled. "That's what I'm trying to find out."

Mitch balled his hands into fists, trying to stay calm. "I ran into her a few weeks ago. She looked pale. Has she been ill?"

"Yes. Every morning for the last several months. She's pregnant."

Chapter Seven

Mitch sat back against his chair with a thump. His napkin drifted to the floor. "Pregnant?"

"Yes. It came as quite a shock to Emma and me, as well. She's due in September. She says the father is out of the picture and won't confirm that it's Bill's, but I suspect it is. The timing would be about right."

Mitch's mouth dried and he swallowed. The baby couldn't be his. The night they'd been together Kristi had said she was on birth control. Had she already been pregnant and not known it?

"While I agree with not telling Bill and bringing him back into our lives, I don't like the idea of my daughter being a single mother. Yet she's determined to have this baby and raise it by herself."

"I can understand your concern." Mitch had seen how much his parents relied on each other and couldn't imagine how hard it would be to raise a child alone.

"I wish she would at least consider resigning from her position to stay home with the baby. She certainly doesn't need the income. I've already moved her cousin

Brett into her department. With some training he should
be able to run things."

Mitch's mouth dropped open. "You're already planning to replace her?"

Larry had the decency to look sheepish. "I only want
what's best for her. She has no idea how difficult things
can be."

"It certainly won't be easy," Mitch agreed.

"She obviously likes and trusts you, or you wouldn't
have lasted as long as you did as her PA. I need your
help. I want you to convince her to resign, or to at least
take a leave of absence."

"Sir, I hardly see her. Haven't for months."

"I've taken care of that. As of Monday I'm bringing
Kristi into the contract negotiations team. She'll be
there to watch Jensen's back. During the last go-round
a few years ago, the union went on strike. They made us
out to be the Big Bad Wolf. The only thing that saved us
was Kristi's quick thinking. Well, that and the bars ran
out of beer and the public got mad. Public sentiment is
fickle."

"True." Without Jensen Distributors putting delivery
trucks on the streets, no alcohol would be arriving at
bars, restaurants and stores. It was a fact both sides were
well aware of.

"There is another reason for her to step aside. This
is not L.A. People of Kristi's stature in our social circle
don't have babies without the benefit of first being
married. She'll be a source of gossip the moment she
starts to show."

Mitch highly doubted that. St. Louis wasn't without its share of scandals. Kristi's pregnancy might be big news for a day or two before something juicier came along.

"But my main concern," Larry continued, "is that her mother had several miscarriages and one stillbirth. Emma wasn't under half the stress Kristi is. I don't want anything happening to my daughter or her baby. Her job is too intense. The risk is too great."

Mitch didn't want anything to happen, either.

"May I think about this?" Mitch asked.

"That's fine. But say yes and there's a huge bonus in it for you. I'll also move you back to the Communications Department. You can be second to Brett. That's a pretty big step up for you."

It was. "Thank you, sir."

"Whatever your decision, Kristi can never learn of our discussion. How about we meet for lunch tomorrow? You can tell me then. Eleven-thirty, my office."

Mitch reached for his phone and entered the appointment into the device's calendar.

"This is a great opportunity for you, Mitch. A win-win for both of us. Heck, if you can find her a husband I'll triple the bonus."

Although it sounded as if Larry was joking, his statement made Mitch pause. "You don't think she should marry for love?"

Larry froze, his arm midair as he motioned for the check. "Kristi's had twenty years to find true love. She hasn't succeeded or even come close. Her mother and I aren't getting any younger. We don't want her alone. A nice guy with the right connections might be the best she can expect at this point."

The waiter arrived with the bill, and Mitch used the diversion as an opportunity to go to the men's room. The situation was ludicrous. He should be saying no way in hell. Kristi was independent, her own woman. Now her father wanted her out of the company because she was pregnant. She'd always claimed he was old-fashioned. Mitch had finally seen Larry Jensen's chauvinism up close.

He walked out with Larry and they parted in the parking lot.

Mitch started the engine. Then he reached into his pocket and retrieved his cell phone. Kristi deserved better than being sideswiped. The phone rang once before it connected. "Hello?"

"Hi, Kristi, it's Mitch. We need to talk."

KRISTI STARED out her living-room window, watching for headlights. Her condo had a great view of the street.

When a man said the words "We need to talk," the conversation never contained good news. Her nerves heightened as another set of headlights rounded the curve, and then she exhaled as the SUV shot past. Not Mitch.

But he was on his way. He hadn't given her any details, just told her he'd had dinner with her father.

Had he found out about the baby?

Another pair of headlights lit up the night, but this set slowed as the four-door sedan rounded the bend and drew to a stop in front of her minuscule yard. A car door slammed and within seconds, her doorbell buzzed.

Kristi turned the dead bolt and opened the door. A cold gust of air blew in despite the fact that the official start of spring had been a week ago. She shut the door behind Mitch as he began to shed his wool overcoat. He was still dressed in the suit he'd worn to work, although he'd loosened the tie. "Hey. Thanks for seeing me on such short notice."

"You said it was important. Come on in. Can I get you something to drink?"

"I'd love a glass of water."

"Of course. This way."

Mitch followed, the ceramic tile creating a three-foot-wide path as it led past the dining area to the open kitchen. She opened a cabinet and removed a tall tumbler. "So what's so important that it couldn't wait until tomorrow?"

"You're joining the negotiations team Monday and your father's training Brett to run your department."

Kristi's hand slipped a little as she pressed the glass to the ice-machine dispenser lever. "No. He wouldn't do that to me."

"He is. He told me tonight."

"Oh." Kristi contemplated this as she filled the glass. This clinched it. Her dad was committed to forcing her out.

Mitch took the water and drained about a third,

giving her a fascinating display of how his lips wrapped around the edge of the glass. Her body remembered his kisses as if they'd occurred yesterday.

"What else does my father want you to do?"

"He wants me to pressure you to resign."

Kristi pressed a second glass against the dispenser and the water shot forth. Her hand shook. "Tell me this is just a bad dream and I'm about to wake up."

When she turned around he was leaning against the counter. "I wish it was."

She drank the water, trying to calm her shaky nerves. "Great. I have handled myself for all these years, but my archaic father can't seem to get it through his head that I'm a big girl. Why does he meddle in my life?"

"Because he cares? Because he went through your mother's miscarriages and that makes him worry about you?"

"He told you I'm pregnant." Her anger boiled as her stress increased.

Mitch had the decency to look her in the face. "Yes."

"Lovely. So much for privacy."

"Hey, I'm on your side here," Mitch said. He sighed. "Look, I'm finding myself in the middle of a place I don't want to be. Your dad thinks I have some sort of influence over you. He thinks I can convince you to resign."

The irony of the situation had Kristi bubbling with hysterical laughter. "And you couldn't say no to the bonus he offered you."

Mitch frowned. "I haven't agreed to anything. We're meeting tomorrow for lunch. If he finds out I'm here I'll probably get fired. I promised him I wouldn't say anything to you."

She resisted the urge to pace. "He's outdone himself this time. He couldn't sit by and do nothing. He couldn't trust me to take care of my health or my life."

"That's why I'm here. I thought you should know what he was up to."

She took a deep, calming breath. Mitch had strong moral fiber, which was one of the things she'd always liked about him. "And I appreciate that."

"So what do we do?"

She thought a moment. "Nothing."

"That's not possible."

"It is. Go to him tomorrow and tell him that you'll do it."

Mitch's forehead creased. "What?"

"You have to buy me some time. I love my job. I need time to prove to him I can cope. If nothing else, I'll convince him that you're looking after me. He'll buy that. He won't fire you if he figures you're acting in my best interests."

"What happens when you don't resign?"

"My dad reconsiders things all the time. If I show him I can manage both my job and the pregnancy, he'll back down. You won't get fired. You might not get a bonus, but you'll have your job."

She refilled his water glass and their fingers touched briefly, sending a tingle up her arm. She noticed Mitch's eyes darken, but he shook his head and took a sip of his water before saying, "So there *was* something wrong in the stairwell. You're having a bad first trimester, aren't you? That's why you're so pale."

"Yes. My pregnancy hasn't been very pleasant up to this point."

"My sister Maria had a rough one. And as the second oldest I watched my mom go through six pregnancies. It does get better."

"That's hard to believe when I feel like crap and my Dark Ages father wants me to resign. I know he thinks he's protecting me, but there's no reason to worry. I discussed the situation with my doctor and she says everything is normal."

"Well, I'm here now. I'll help you through this."

"Thanks." Mitch always had understood her. Maybe having him around wouldn't be such a bad thing. She wished she could tell him he was the baby's father, but her dad was already being impossible and she didn't want Mitch to lose his job.

Plus, if Mitch learned he was the father, he would insist on doing the right thing. He would want to marry her out of a sense of responsibility, not because he couldn't live without her. And that girl he'd claimed to love? Kristi would be denying him his chance to win her. Mitch deserved to marry for love, not obligation.

"My father is a meddler," she declared, "but I'm not going to let him run my life. Tomorrow tell him yes. It'll buy me a few months to change his mind. I'll make sure he doesn't fire you. If I have to, I'll threaten never to speak with him again."

"He's just worried."

"He's trying to control me. He wants me to stay home and play house like this is the 1950s. Well, it's not."

She saw hesitation in his eyes. "Do this for me. Please."

It was the plea that got him—he nodded. Kristi sighed with relief and impulsively gave Mitch a hug.

As his arms closed around her, Kristi's breath caught in her throat. She'd heard pregnancy hormones heightened your senses, and now she was experiencing it first-hand.

Mitch wore the same cologne as he had the night he'd made love to her. A light five-o'clock shadow framed his sexy lips.

Her body began to hum, recognizing the man who'd brought her to bliss and beyond. She struggled to control her racing heart and disentangled herself from his embrace before she did something stupid like kiss him. "Sorry."

"Don't apologize. I didn't mind."

He stepped away, giving her much-needed space.

"I've always appreciated the way you respect me," she said, trying to slow her breathing.

He nodded. "I do. Very much. You realize, though, we're going to have to work closely together."

"Yes."

"As long as you're okay with that."

"I can handle it," she said, although really, she wasn't

sure that she could. It would be hard to keep a professional distance.

"Good, because this time, you won't be my boss."

HIS SISTER WOULD AGAIN call him an idiot, but for the first time, Kristi was available, and she needed him. He'd be there for her. Maybe he could even win her heart.

Heck, Larry had practically given his blessing. Okay, maybe that was a stretch. But the door was open a crack, and Mitch intended to take full advantage. He leaned closer, and Kristi's lips parted. He wanted nothing more than to kiss her, but he had to take things slow or he'd scare her off for sure.

Somehow he spoke. "I need to go before I kiss you."

A RUSH OF DISAPPOINTMENT took Kristi by surprise. She'd wanted him to kiss her.

He stepped forward. "Are you okay?"

"I think I need to sit down."

He reached for her arm and guided her to a sofa. "Wait here."

He returned with a box of crackers and a glass of clear, bubbly soda. "These should help."

"What'll help is getting my dad off my case." He frowned. "I know. I know. I'm fixated."

Mitch sat at the other end of the sofa and watched while she dug out a cracker. She bit it in half and washed it down with soda. "I promise to focus on only good things."

"I'm happy to hear that." His smile warmed her insides, and Kristi knew she was in trouble. One night had affected her more than she'd ever imagined.

"So, this won't put a cramp in your style, will it?"

"What do you mean?"

"Um, you know. Babysitting me for my dad. It won't hurt your social life."

He chuckled. "I'll manage."

"So how are things working out with that girl? The one you really liked."

Mitch bobbed his head and the corners of his lips inched upward. "She knows who I am now. I'm making some progress."

"Oh, that's great." Kristi forced herself to sound thrilled. Mitch's heart was taken. All they'd shared was lust.

"I think so, too." He grinned.

Kristi covered her disappointment with a big gulp of soda and another cracker.

In the living room, the grandfather clock that had been a housewarming present from her parents began to chime. "If you're better, I'll take off. How about we meet up after work and I'll let you know how lunch with your dad went?"

"Sure."

"I'll call you." Mitch rose, and seeing her shift, shook his head. "You stay there. I can show myself out."

"I'm fine." Kristi got to her feet and followed him.

She stood there awkwardly as Mitch put on his coat and opened the door. After an exchange of "good night," he left.

She shut the front door behind him and watched from the window as he climbed into his car. The overhead light illuminated him briefly, and then she heard the engine roar before the low beams cut a swath through the night. Mitch's taillights soon faded into the developing fog.

She wrapped her arms around herself and sat on the living-room couch. Her father wanted her to resign. Her hormones were out of control. Mitch's dream girl was starting to notice him—she should be happy about that, but she wasn't.

Only one thing was for sure.

Sparks were nothing but trouble.

Chapter Eight

"So that's the story." Kristi summed up the situation for Alison over lunch. She tried to ignore the fact that at this moment Mitch was dining with her father.

Alison whistled low. She'd been listening intently for the last ten minutes as Kristi related the events of the previous evening. "Wow. I never seriously thought your dad would go this far."

"What, you thought he'd stop?" Kristi tapped her fingers on the table in a rapid staccato. They'd escaped the office to eat at their favorite bistro. "Luckily Mitch told me about all this."

"What if Mitch finds out the baby is his?"

"He won't. He can't. Besides, his dream girl is starting to realize he's alive. It's not fair to keep him from true love."

"A noble cause if it exists." Alison stabbed some salad.

"It does, I'm sure of it." At least she prayed there was such a thing.

"I hope you're right for both of our sakes."

Kristi nodded. "Me, too."

"Are you okay? You're looking paler than usual," Alison said.

"I haven't been sleeping very well. I'm stressed." Kristi took her napkin and wiped her lips.

"Think of your insomnia as preparation for the night feedings ahead. Has Dr. Krasnoff checked your blood levels yet?"

Kristi shook her head. "That's at my next appointment. Why?"

"Carrying Kelsey made me anemic. I had to take iron supplements the entire pregnancy. Low iron could be what's making you feel run-down and blue."

Kristi nodded. As a strong and confident woman, she rarely found herself totally overwhelmed. She'd learned to handle anything, from business crises to personal rejections. She bounced back. She remained in control. Having a baby had changed everything.

"So you're seeing Mitch tonight?"

"Yes. We're meeting after work. He's cooking me dinner at his place."

Alison frowned. "That sounds personal."

"Where else are we going to talk? Just because I'm on the negotiating team come Monday doesn't mean we can be seen hanging out. We don't work together like we used to. His place sounds safe and, believe me, I'm not up for doing any cooking."

"Just be careful," Alison warned.

"When am I not?" Kristi replied, and then realizing the implications, she began to laugh. "Don't answer that."

Alison covered her mouth, but failed to suppress the giggles. "Trying not to."

With a shake of her head at the irony, Kristi ate her lunch.

"HI. ANY TROUBLE finding it?" Mitch asked as he opened the door to his St. Louis Hills bungalow. His gaze roved over Kristi, assessing her mood.

She smiled and it lit up her entire face. He relaxed. "Your directions were great. I like your place. It's cute."

It wasn't big, but Mitch didn't need much space.

"Something smells good."

"Baked ravioli. Let me take your coat."

"Okay." She shrugged out of her coat and deposited the garment in Mitch's outstretched hand. Although today had been in the low sixties, a cold front was passing through and there was even a chance for snow flurries. "Wow, you cooked?"

Mitch grinned. "I did. Surprised?"

"A little," Kristi admitted, chuckling.

He moved through an archway and placed her coat on the back of a dining-room chair. "So you're hungry?" Mitch teased as her stomach gave a loud growl.

"I'm always hungry. Now that my appetite's come back, I'm a bottomless pit."

She followed him through a doorway into the small kitchen at the back of the house. Mitch opened the oven, removed the pan and set it on the counter.

"Is there anything I can do to help?" Kristi asked.

"Toss the salad?" he suggested as he took a foil-wrapped garlic bread loaf out of the oven. "It's on the top shelf."

"I can do that." She opened the refrigerator and found an Italian salad. "Did you make this, too?"

"That's from Dierberg's deli." Mitch named a locally owned grocery store chain as he handed Kristi some tongs. She tossed the iceberg and romaine lettuce, sliced red onions, artichoke hearts, croutons and pimentos. The homemade dressing was in a former jelly jar, and she dumped the Italian vinaigrette on the salad, added the Parmesan cheese and tossed again.

"How did you know Italian food was my favorite?" she asked once they were seated at the table.

"I was your PA. It was my job to notice things."

"I wish my current PA was as good. She's wedding obsessed."

Kristi closed her eyes as she savored a morsel of ravioli and Mitch's heart raced. "Wow. This is good stuff. Better than at some of the restaurants where I've eaten."

"Thanks."

"Where did you learn to cook?"

"My mom. With eight kids, she was always cooking."

"I can't imagine that many people. It's always been Mom, my dad and me. Is your family close?"

"We're very tight-knit."

"I always wanted siblings. Was it fun growing up with so many brothers and sisters?"

"It was fun, but chaotic. And I had to be a role model. That was assumed. I couldn't let anyone down."

"That's a lot of pressure to put on a kid."

"Yeah, but it's just part of being in a family, and the love and support I received more than made up for any extra responsibilities."

She ran her hand over her stomach. "I hope my baby won't be an only child."

It was too soon to see much change in Kristi's figure. "Whatever happens, I know she'll be happy and well loved."

Kristi smiled. "Alison swears it's a boy. She says her sisters know these things, even though it's too soon to tell. The doctor said I could find out at the ultrsound I'll have in late April. But I'm not sure I want to know."

"You want to be surprised?" Maria had been determined to learn the sex, and then had decorated the nursery accordingly.

"Part of me does. After all, I was surprised I was pregnant. It'll be rather fitting."

"So the pregnancy was an accident?" His voice hitched at the end of the sentence and Kristi's eyes widened guiltily.

"A baby is always a blessing," she sidestepped.

"You didn't answer my question."

She set her fork down. "It's been a great meal so far. Let's not ruin it by talking about this. I'm having a nice evening, and that's been rare lately."

Mitch sensed there was something she was hiding, but decided not to press. "I agree. So what do you think about the Blues' playoff chances?" He knew she liked professional hockey. His topic choice was a good one, and they had a rousing discussion.

"You know, you should put in for some corporate tickets," Kristi said. "They're great seats. Right on center ice. Does your dream girl like hockey?"

"Yes."

"Then you should get tickets and ask her to the game. Or take your dad. I bet he would like to go."

"My dad probably would." Mitch rose. "I hope you left some room. There's dessert."

She leaned back and put her hands over her stomach. "You're kidding me. Really?"

"Nope. You'll like this."

"It's been so good already." He brought out two forks, two plates, a small foil pie pan, a knife and a can of whipped cream. "I also have vanilla ice cream if you want."

"This is fine." She noticed the brand. "Ooh. Tippin's."

"Yeah, this is my secret indulgence. Don't tell anyone, but I'm a sucker for apple pie."

The pie served four, and Mitch cut them each a slice. He shook the whipped cream, turned the can upside down and sprayed a big blob that foamed over the top and down the sides of one piece of pie.

Mitch paused. "I usually have the ice cream. That's not as pretty as it looks on the commercial."

Kristi stood. "Give me that. Let me show you how to do this."

"Oh, so you're the expert?" Mitch passed her the can and leaned over her shoulder so he could watch.

"You bet I am. I grew up with this stuff." She pressed the nozzle, making a perfect spiral on the other slice.

"Okay, you win. It was my first attempt."

She swiveled to face him, canister in hand. "You've never used whipped cream?"

"Not from a can. My mother won't let the fake stuff in the house. She claims it's unhealthy, and makes her own. You should have seen the drama Lauri caused when she brought home a tub of Cool Whip."

"Canned whipped cream is great. Here. I'll show you. Open wide," Kristi said.

"What?" Mitch began, and as he spoke, Kristi moved the nozzle close to his face and pressed. The cream shot forth, hitting the inside and the outside of his closing mouth. He jumped back slightly, trying to swallow and using his fingers to stop the cream running down his chin. "Hey!"

"You were supposed to keep your mouth open." Kristi tilted the white tip, and shot cream into her own mouth. "See?"

Mitch wiped the cream off his face and pressed a residual dollop onto Kristi's nose. "You are a menace."

"It's not intentional."

"Still." He used his thumb to wipe some whipped cream from her nose.

"That tickled."

"Did it? Eat your pie." With a thump he sat in his

chair. Anything to keep from kissing Kristi, as he'd wanted to when he'd wiped the cream from her nose. He deliberately shoved a chunk into his mouth and then pointed. "Try some."

"Sure." But Kristi seemed subdued. She smeared the perfect spiral into an unshapely blob on the top of her pie. She then stabbed the point with her fork and shoved the portion into her mouth.

She was angry and he wasn't exactly sure why.

"So what did my dad say today?" she asked.

Ah, so maybe that was it. "He was thrilled that I accepted his offer."

"Figures." She stabbed the pie again.

He gestured to her plate with his fork. "You don't have to kill it."

"I'm frustrated."

"I can see that. Why?"

"I don't want to talk about it. Tell me the status of the negotiations. That way I'm up to speed on Monday."

Mitch knew when not to press, and he spent the next half hour filling her in. "So what have you left for Brett?"

"Nothing he can damage. I'll go by my office every morning and afternoon to check on things, and technically in my absence Mark's in charge. Brett's too green. But he's smart and will catch on quickly. The longer these negotiations drag on, the harder it will be for me to get my department back. And you know that's what my dad wants."

"He only wants you to be happy. Deep down, that is his motivation."

Kristi's cell phone began to ring. "Speak of the devil himself."

Mitch stood to give her privacy. "Go ahead. Answer. I'll clean the table."

ALTHOUGH HE WAS the last person she wanted to talk to, Kristi answered the call. "Hi, Dad."

"Hey, Kristi." Her father sounded smug, she decided. She forced herself to remain calm. "Where are you?"

"Actually, I'm at Mitch's. He cooked me dinner—baked ravioli."

"Really?"

Don't sound so gleeful, Kristi thought. "Yes. He suggested dinner so that I could be brought up to speed regarding the contract negotiations."

"He's a smart one. What a great idea. I had lunch with him today."

"He mentioned it."

"He did?" Her father was fishing, and she gave him what he wanted.

"Yes. He said you were picking his brain since his father's in a union."

"That's right. I wanted to hear from someone who's lived it. Up until now we've just been relying on our consultants."

Mitch came through to get more plates. Kristi rolled her eyes and he smiled sympathetically.

"So is there a reason you called?" she asked.

"Actually, yes. Your mother and I have been invited to dinner at the club tomorrow with Hannah and Reginald Ivey. Their son is in town. We thought you could round out the dinner party and make it even numbers."

"Dad."

"Kristi, he's divorced and has kids. He already knows you're pregnant."

"Dad, I know you and Mom mean well, but really, enough. No more matchmaking."

"You aren't going to find anyone without help."

That got her. She bristled. "Actually, I already have."

Anything to make the incessant matchmaking end.

That got her dad's attention and she knew she'd shocked him. "Who? Do I know him?"

"I can't tell you who he is." Uh-oh, she should have thought this through. What had possessed her to go down this path?

"Why not?" her father grew agitated. "Does this guy really even exist?"

"Yes. But you know how you get. You'll crush him like a bug or something if I tell you his name." *Come on, Kristi, think of something.*

"So he works for me?"

"Maybe...."

Her father punctuated each word. "I want to know who he is."

Mitch had walked back into the room. The table was cleared and he folded his arms over his chest. His brow was creased, his eyes quizzical.

"It's Mitch!" Too late, she slapped a hand over her mouth.

"What!" She held the phone away from her ear. Oh, crap.

She had to salvage the situation as best she could. She ignored Mitch's stricken expression. She'd make it up to him somehow. "Dad, he cooked me dinner. He's really an attractive guy. And I'm not his boss anymore. Why shouldn't I go out with him?"

"You won't date Mitch. He's an employee."

"So? You like him. Why does his job matter?"

"You're about to be spending tons of time with him."

"It'll give us a chance to get to know each other. Even better."

"I'll…I'll—"

"You won't fire him or I'll testify against you in court myself. If you don't want us together, you can send me back to my department, and Mark or Brett can handle the PR angle."

"So that's what this is really about." Kristi heard her dad sputter.

"Dad, I'm a grown woman and I'll date who I want."

She chuckled as her dad hung up on her. She flipped the phone closed. Mitch had whitened, which was near-impossible as his skin was permanently sun-kissed. "You told him you were interested in me?"

"Yeah… Sorry, he and my mom are once again trying to marry me off."

"You didn't even ask me if you could get me into this."

"No, and I really am sorry, but maybe it's the perfect solution. The more he thinks about it, the more he'll want us apart. I could be back in my department by Monday morning. And you'd be free from his scheming."

Mitch yanked a hand through his hair. "I don't know, Kristi. This might backfire in a major way."

Kristi winced. She'd opened a really big can of worms. Worse, she hadn't even thought of Mitch's feelings. "I really screwed up, didn't I? I'll figure out a way to fix it. I promise."

Guilt overtook her and hot tears prickled her eyes. She stood up.

Mitch was immediately at her side and he gathered her into his arms. "Hey, it'll be okay."

"No, it won't. My whole life has become one big, giant mess." Months of changing hormones had her weeping and tears dripped onto his shirt. He lifted her chin.

"It's not that bad and not worth crying over. I don't mind. As long as I don't lose my job, the world won't end."

She'd never realized how much she'd taken for granted. "Your job is really that important. I mean, not just because you like it or have to pay the bills. It's more than that."

Pressed chest to chest, she felt the vibrations of his exhale. "My dad's been out of work for a year. I've been quietly slipping him money to pay the bills. My mom doesn't know that I've been helping. I don't want her to worry about the money. And I want Lauri to have the best wedding possible."

"You are a good man. Whoever that girl is, she's stupid if she doesn't realize how perfect you are."

Mitch tightened his grip. "No, she's not."

She shook her head. "It's not right that I dragged you into this. I'll tell my dad the truth tomorrow."

"No, don't."

Kristi blinked. "Are you sure?"

He nodded. "Yep. You started this, but I'm okay with it. Let's let it play out. Things might work the way you want, with your father loosening up and sending you back to your old job."

"You'd do that for me?"

"We're friends, aren't we?"

She reached out to touch his face. "You constantly surprise me."

He smiled. "If you don't stop the compliments, you'll enlarge my ego so much that my sisters will feel the need to take me down a few pegs."

"Sorry." A strange shyness overtook her. This was Mitch. She'd worked with him, kissed him and spent the night in his arms, but tonight had proved that she didn't really know him. Perhaps she should get to know him better. After all, he was the father of her child.

Chapter Nine

Mitch folded his hands in his lap and tried to project an air of calm. Larry Jensen's secretary picked up the phone. "Mr. Jensen will see you now."

After a twenty-minute wait, Mitch was finally ushered into the CEO's inner sanctum. Here the carpet was plush, the paneling mahogany and the leather rich. No expense had been spared; even the artwork was original.

Larry remained seated and motioned Mitch toward a chair in front of his desk. Mitch sat and readied himself.

"How did dinner go?" Larry asked without preamble.

"We discussed business and I brought her up to speed. She's not happy being moved to the negotiations team, but Kristi's a fighter."

"She is." Larry seemed pleased by that fact, Mitch noted, although the reprieve was fleeting. "What is your timetable to get her to resign?"

"Sir, I just began."

"Can the *sir*. Makes me feel old. Hell, maybe I am old."

Larry's gaze narrowed. "Last night my daughter told me she's interested in you. To say I'm a little bit concerned is an understatement."

Mitch's surprise wasn't faked. While Larry never minced words, he hadn't expected him to be quite so blunt. "Oh."

"That's all you have to say?"

Being a double agent in real life was harder than it looked on TV. "I'm not really sure what to tell you."

"Do you like my daughter?"

"She was a wonderful boss."

Larry snorted. "That's not what I mean and you know it. She's using you to get back at me. She's mad so she's decided to date someone I won't approve of."

Mitch tried to bite down a retort. Just because he came from a large South Side blue-collar family did not mean he was a social pariah. "I can promise you that I won't touch her." *Again,* Mitch amended to himself.

"No, that's the opposite of what I want you to do."

"Sir?" Mitch caught himself. "Mr. Jensen?"

"Larry. No, here's the new plan. If she wants to date you, go out with her. Tell her I gave you my blessing. It'll drive her nuts."

Mitch had never seen a father-daughter relationship so convoluted. He knew they loved each other dearly, but they were both far too stubborn for their own good. And he was now clearly in the thick of it all.

"What if things progress?"

Larry shrugged, unconcerned. "I doubt Kristi's going to keep you around that long, Mitch. She's using you as a smoke screen to get her mother and me to stop matchmaking. Once we start accepting you into the family fold, she'll run for the hills. I'm amending our deal. Let her work until she gives birth. If you can get her to stay home permanently once the baby's here, you can have your pick of jobs."

Mitch had the sudden impression he was far out of his league. He'd agreed to Kristi's scheme mainly because it would give him a chance to win her over. Now her father had upped the ante. Kristi wasn't going to like this.

As for Mitch, the girl of his dreams had been handed to him on a silver platter—sort of—but this wasn't the way he wanted things.

The door to Larry's office burst open with a slam that vibrated several objects on a nearby shelf.

"Don't you dare fire him." Kristi glared at her father as she entered the room. "I can't believe you'd do this."

"Do what? You told me you liked him, so I called him up here to lay down the ground rules for dating my daughter. That's what any good father would do."

She planted her hands on her hips, the shirt she was wearing tightened, revealing a stomach beginning to round. "I can run my own social life."

Larry stood and walked over to his daughter. He placed a hand on Mitch's chair. "Yes, but Mitch is too valuable an employee to lose. Marvin thinks the world of him, and I figured, why not give him a chance? Your mother will be thrilled you've met someone."

Kristi's mouth dropped open. "So you're saying you're okay with this? My dating Mitch."

"Why wouldn't I be? He has an MBA and tons of potential. I can see why you're falling for him."

It was like watching one of those scenes where you wanted to look away, but kept staring, because if you didn't you might miss something important. Kristi wasn't good at reining in her emotions, and everything from rage to shock flickered across her face. Her dad had called her bluff and this was something she hadn't prepared for.

Larry didn't let Kristi speak. "I'm going to call your mother and tell her the good news. How about dinner at the club tonight? I'm sure she'll want to meet Mitch in this new context. We should get to know him personally, right?"

Mitch stood then, seeing an opening. "Larry—" Kristi's eyes widened at his familiar use of her dad's name "—how about we do dinner later in the week? This is all new to us and I'd like some time to romance Kristi properly."

Larry nodded as he went behind his desk. "I can live with that. See how smart he is?"

Mitch dropped his arm on Kristi's shoulder. She looked shaken. "Do you mind if I take Kristi for some food and we can continue this later?" he asked.

"No need. We're good. In fact, why don't you take

the day off? Both of you. Go have some fun. The weather's finally turned."

As Larry picked up the phone, Mitch guided Kristi into the hallway and down to her office. She started yelling the moment he safely shut the door behind them.

"He's a demon. He… He…" She began to hyperventilate, and Mitch helped her into a chair. She buried her head in her hands. "He wasn't supposed to go for this."

"I know." Mitch ran his fingers through her hair in a soothing motion.

"I'm a horrible person."

"No, you're not." Mitch inhaled her floral scent and sighed. Life had gotten so complicated. It should be so easy. Meet, fall in love, live happily ever after. "Why don't we play along with your father for a while?"

"What about your dream girl? I can't ruin things between you."

Mitch continued to stroke her hair and she leaned into him. "Maybe it'll make her jealous. Make her wake up and see me for who I really am, a guy who's crazy about her."

"She's a fool for not knowing that already."

Mitch kissed the top of Kristi's head. Silly thing. Someday he'd tell her the truth, but not yet. No need to play all his cards too soon. He'd loved Kristi for far too long to blow this chance to win her heart.

"So what do you say we take your dad's advice? It's

nearly eighty out there and sunny. Let's go to Forest Park."

"I haven't played hooky from work in years."

Mitch grinned. "Then it's time you did."

THEIR FIRST STOP was the St. Louis Zoo. Located off Hampton, the zoo consisted of ninety landscaped acres.

"It seems like everyone else has the same idea," Mitch said as a couple passed them on the raised walkway of the 1904 free-flight bird cage. Kristi watched while a bird landed. Then she and Mitch wandered their way to the structure's south exit, neither in any hurry. All around, mothers pushed strollers, and young children shouted when they saw animals they liked.

"Still upset about your dad?" Mitch asked.

She nodded. "Why does he do this? Why can't he act like a normal father?"

"I don't know. I can't say my dad is normal, either."

"Compared to mine he has to be." They passed the giraffes as they made their way toward Big Cat Country. She leaned over to look at the leopards. They lay around with nothing to do. "I can understand how you feel, buddy."

"What do you mean?"

"Trapped. This is their life." She indicated the third-of-an acre habitat the animals inhabited.

"So you feel trapped?"

She shouldn't have brought it up. "It's my mess and I'll fix it. But yeah, sometimes being me isn't all it's cracked up to be. Poor little rich girl. Sounds so pitiful, doesn't it? But despite all the privileges I had growing up, I worked hard to get where I am at Jensen. My job is important to me. I don't want anyone taking that away."

"It's not all of who you are. You might find that things change when you hold your child in your arms."

Kristi couldn't see that happening, and switched subjects by pointing out the lions. All the animals were enjoying spring's arrival.

"It's hard to believe Easter is around the corner," Mitch remarked.

"Does your family do anything special?" Kristi asked.

"We go to church on Saturday night and have brunch at my parents' house at noon the next day. My parents took us to a sunrise service once when we were little, but once most of us were teens we wanted to sleep in. You?"

"We usually go to Palm Springs. That's where my mom's parents retired."

"Sounds fun."

"Not really. Brunch at the club. See and be seen."

"No one in your family cooks?"

She shook her head. "No."

He dropped an arm over her shoulder, a friendly gesture and one she liked. "I'll have to teach you to cook. But first, let's eat lunch."

They left the zoo, but not Forest Park, and ate at the Boathouse, which was a new structure designed to resemble early-twentieth-century Midwestern boat-houses. Their table overlooked the lake. "Should we rent a paddleboat?" Mitch asked as they polished off some chocolate cake.

"I've never been out on this lake."

"Neither have I, which means we have to go."

Although the paddleboats looked like fun, they opted instead for the familiarity of a rowboat. The day was perfect, and the hour-long journey gave them fantastic views of the St. Louis Art Museum, the World's Fair pavilion, a few turtles and several flocks of migrating geese.

"That was fun," Mitch said as he rowed them back to the dock.

"You see people go rowing in movies all the time and we forget we can do it right here in St. Louis. Now where to?"

"Your choice," Mitch replied. They ended up visiting the art museum before strolling along the bike path.

What was important, though, was that they talked. She found Mitch just as easy to get along with outside the office as inside. "So tomorrow, how do we handle things?"

Mitch paused and an in-line skater went by. "What do you mean?"

"About us. This dating fiasco we've gotten ourselves into. You know how gossip spreads at work."

"Let them talk."

"I'm worried about that," she admitted.

"Why? We can pull it off. We may have to kiss,

but you didn't mind my kisses the night of the Christmas party, did you? Surely you could tolerate a few more…"

He smiled devilishly, and Kristi's heart fluttered. She had enjoyed his kisses. "Uh, they were okay," she downplayed.

"Just okay?" Mitch's grin widened as he recognized her lie. "Then we'll have to work on that. It's been a few months."

"Oh, that's not necessary," Kristi began, but Mitch's mouth lowered anyway.

His lips were firm but gentle and he had that indescribable primal male appeal that would make even the most levelheaded woman swoon. She fought to keep her eyes open, but lost the battle as her lids fluttered closed and a zing began to race through her bloodstream. A light breeze cooled her heated skin, reminding her they were outside in the bright sunlight, in view of everyone.

She reveled in the sweetness and passion of the moment, savoring every touch until Mitch lifted his lips from hers. "There. That wasn't so bad, was it?"

"Tolerable," she managed to say, not wanting him to realize how much he'd affected her. She blinked as her eyes readjusted to the bright sunlight. "It'll do."

"Good," Mitch said. He assessed her for a moment, male satisfaction evident in his gleaming brown eyes. "I wouldn't want us to have to fake that."

"Oh, we won't."

"We might need to kiss more. Make certain we're really comfortable with it."

"Uh, not a good idea."

Mitch's eyes twinkled. "Okay, come on. We should get going anyway. If I know you, you're going to want to check your e-mail and clean out your in-box before you go home."

She winced. "Am I that predictable?"

"Yes, but it's not a bad thing."

But later, as she checked her e-mail, Kristi wasn't so sure.

"THIS IS BAD. Very bad." Alison shook her head and paced Kristi's office, which made two of them walking in circles later that evening, after Mitch and Kristi's lunch date. "How can you go out with Mitch?"

"I already told you."

"Yeah, but I'm still having trouble believing you'd do something this stupid."

"Don't hold back," Kristi replied bitterly.

"I won't. Kristi, you opened Pandora's box. Nothing can go back in. If Mitch finds out he's the father of your child, he'll ask you to marry him."

"Well, I won't. I don't want to be with someone who's marrying me out of a sense of obligation."

"You're already on a hormonal roller coaster. What are you going to do if you fall in love with him?"

"I won't," Kristi insisted, although doubt crept in.

"Well, what if you do?"

"I'll cross that bridge when I come to it," Kristi replied stubbornly.

"You, the planner, not have a plan? That's how you got yourself into this mess."

Kristi rubbed her temples and took a seat. She had a headache. "The only reason I asked you to drop by tonight was so you'd hear my news before the grapevine fires up first thing tomorrow. I didn't need a lecture."

"So what were his kisses like?"

"Wonderful."

Alison pounced. "Aha! You're already falling for him."

"We've always had chemistry." Kristi rubbed her stomach. She couldn't believe how her body was changing. She'd already had to buy new underwear and pants. Her pumps were starting to feel tight, as well, and she'd read that her foot could increase by at least one shoe size.

Alison flopped into an empty chair. "I have no idea what to tell you. I guess just take things one day at a time."

"I'm trying. Believe me, I'm trying."

"AND I THOUGHT THAT we'd do the wedding reception…" Mitch tuned out his sister Lauri as she prattled on about wedding plans. It was now Easter, and down the table, Mitch caught his brother Nick's amused gaze.

"More lamb?" Kate asked.

"That'd be great." Mitch took the platter from his

sister. The family had been at the house since 10:00 a.m., and now it was a little past five.

"So how are negotiations going?" his father asked.

"They aren't," Mitch told him. "The contract expires in two weeks, so we're down to the wire."

He'd seen Kristi daily since their date, although they hadn't had a real date since. In that past two weeks, they'd been working fifteen-hour days. He'd taken her to dinner, usually after she'd gone back to her office and done all her e-mail. Trying to maintain her grip on Brett and the negotiations was taking its toll. She was tired. Everyone on the team was.

"I'm glad I'm not in your shoes," his father said, spooning some more green beans onto his plate.

At that moment, Mitch's cell phone vibrated. He pulled the phone from his pocket and read the number. His mouth dried. "Excuse me."

Going into the kitchen, Mitch answered the call. As soon as he said hello, he could hear Kristi's sobbing. "Hey. What's wrong?"

"Something's wrong with the baby."

"I'm on my way."

Sensing movement, Mitch turned around. Maria had followed him into the kitchen. She held up an empty baby bottle. "Jane's out of formula. So you're leaving?"

He slipped his phone into this jeans pocket. "It's an emergency."

"Whose? Wait. Don't tell me. This is déjà vu. You're leaving a family dinner to help Kristi Jensen."

Mitch could still hear Kristi's tears. "She's in trouble."

Maria followed him into the utility room, where Mitch grabbed his car keys from the Peg-Board his father had long ago installed to keep things from getting lost.

"You aren't her PA anymore, Mitch. You can't keep racing to her rescue every time she calls you. How are you ever going to find a girlfriend?"

Mitch turned the door handle and tossed the cryptic words back over his shoulder. "She *is* my girlfriend."

Chapter Ten

Kristi paced her condo, hugging her stomach. She hadn't planned on calling Mitch. But her parents were out of town in Palm Springs for the holiday, and Alison had Easter bunny activities planned with her kids.

She'd called the physician's exchange. "Dr. Krasnoff is at the hospital delivering a baby," the nurse had said. "I'll be alerting her you're on your way in."

Consumed with fear, the moment she'd disconnected Kristi had dialed Mitch. As he had many times during a work-related crisis, he would make things better. He arrived within twenty minutes.

"Hey, I'm here. It's going to be okay."

"I'm spotting. The book says this might be bad. Very bad."

He pulled her into his arms and kissed her forehead. "Let's get you to the doctor. Did you call her?"

Kristi hiccupped. "She's at St. John's delivering a baby. I'm supposed to meet her there."

"Then that's where we're going."

St. John's was five minutes away, and the exchange had alerted the E.R. of her arrival. Kristi was quickly moved to the maternity ward, where a nurse helped her into a gown and took her vitals.

"Dr. Krasnoff is finishing up and will be in shortly." The nurse patted Kristi's shoulder. "It won't be long at all."

Mitch reached for Kristi's hand. "You and the baby are going to be fine."

Kristi turned her face toward his. "My mother had three miscarriages before she had me. I can't lose this baby."

"You won't." Mitch tightened his grip. "Right now you just need to concentrate on relaxing."

Kristi exhaled some stress. Mitch always calmed her down. "I'm glad you're here."

At that moment the doctor entered. "Hi, Kristi. Sorry it took me a minute. I had to change scrubs." Dr. Krasnoff sanitized her hands again. "What's going on?"

Her lip quivered. "I'm spotting."

"Okay, before we panic, let's take a look."

The nurse stepped into the room. "Bring me the ultrasound machine," Dr. Krasnoff told her. The nurse nodded and left, and Dr. Krasnoff glanced at Mitch, but directed her words to Kristi. "And this is?"

"Mitch. He's…" She faltered. She couldn't tell Mitch he was the father now, not under these circumstances.

"I'm her boyfriend," Mitch completed. "I plan to be her labor coach."

"Kristi, is it fine if he stays?"

"Yes. I want him here."

Dr. Krasnoff nodded at Mitch. "Stand up near her shoulders so I have room to do the exam. Okay, Kristi, you know the drill."

The nurse arrived with the ultrasound and helped get Kristi's feet in the stirrups. She also covered her with a warm blanket. Dr. Krasnoff examined Kristi's cervix, and then she covered Kristi's lower half and had her lie flat with only her stomach exposed. Then Dr. Krasnoff fired up the ultrasound machine, squirted the gel and began to press the wand on Kristi's stomach. "Let's see what baby's doing."

The black screen came alive with white curves and lines. "There's the baby and that's a good heartbeat." Dr. Krasnoff moved the wand more as the baby became clearly visible. "Now let's check your placenta. Did you have any pain or cramping with this spotting?"

"No." Kristi watched the image on the screen. She'd glimpsed eyes, a mouth and a hand as Dr. Krasnoff searched. "Why?"

"Cramping could mean placental abruption. That's when the placenta separates from the uterine wall. Ah, there it is."

Kristi didn't have any idea what Dr. Krasnoff was searching for, but a few seconds later she lifted the wand and the nurse turned off the machine. "Am I okay?"

Dr. Krasnoff wiped the gel off Kristi's stomach. "I don't see anything of concern. What were you doing when you started spotting?"

"I'd been moving furniture out of the second bedroom so that I can turn it into a nursery."

Dr. Krasnoff nodded. "That could cause spotting, especially if you were pushing with your stomach or your backside. Were you straining or exerting yourself?"

"Maybe." Kristi tried to remember.

"Well, to be on the safe side, here's what you're going to do. You don't need bed rest, but you do have to make a few changes. You can work, but no exercise, no strenuous movement of any kind, especially furniture moving, and no sex. Sorry, boyfriend."

"It's okay," Mitch said. He'd been holding Kristi's hand, and he gave it a squeeze.

"I want to recheck you every two weeks from here on out. However, if you spot again, you call me immediately like you did today. I'd much rather check and find nothing than be sorry, especially with your family history. Hopefully this will be a onetime deal."

"I hope so, too." Relief flooded Kristi and happy tears gathered in her eyes. Until she'd faced the idea of losing her child, she hadn't realized how important her baby had become. She already loved her child. Today she'd discovered she had maternal instincts, and they'd kicked in full force.

"You can get dressed and go home as soon as the nurse gives you your discharge papers." Dr. Krasnoff paused in the doorway. "Remember what I said. Leave the heavy stuff to someone else. Don't lift or move anything heavier than a gallon of milk."

"I won't." Now that the enormity of the moment had passed, the adrenaline letdown caused Kristi to feel like a big idiot. "I can't believe I caused this. I shouldn't have tried to do the nursery."

"You didn't know. My sister built an entire entertainment center, two bookshelves and a microwave cart while carrying Jane. She called her actions nesting."

"That's it, all right. But it was stupid of me."

Mitch helped her off the hospital bed. "Not stupid. Stubborn. You're not alone, though. You have me to help. You heard the doctor. If there are things that you need done I want you to call me."

The nurse reiterated all Dr. Krasnoff's instructions before releasing Kristi. She tucked the papers into her purse, and Mitch drove her home and walked her inside. He glanced around. "You're not celebrating Easter?" he asked.

"I had a few milk-chocolate eggs at lunch."

He frowned. "Where was that?"

"My kitchen."

His brow creased. "I thought you were spending Easter with your parents."

"They're in Palm Springs. I decided not to go."

"You should have told me. You shouldn't be alone on a holiday. Are you up to going somewhere?"

Kristi glanced down. She wore a pretty floral top and some black stretchy pants that Alison had given her. "I guess. Why?"

"Are you hungry?"

In response, her stomach growled. She gave a light, embarrassed laugh. "You know, lately I'm always starving."

"Then join me for dinner. It's Easter and you shouldn't be alone. My mom's cooking."

The offer was sweet and gave her that warm, fuzzy feeling. However... "That's tempting, but I shouldn't intrude."

He grabbed her hands. "They want to meet you. I told them I'm dating you, when I rushed out."

His family knew about her? This ruse was going too far. "I'm tired. I'll be fine here."

"Scared?" He drew her into an embrace.

"Today's been pretty emotional."

"You'll be okay." His lips were close and tempting, within kissing range. She was highly aware of him, especially when he gave her a cajoling grin. "Come to my house. Take a break and forget for a while. My mom made lamb. I can't even describe how good it is."

Her mouth watered. Unless she wanted fast food, most restaurants had closed after they'd served brunch.

"Give me a few minutes."

After Kristi freshened up, Mitch drove them into the city and parked in front of a sprawling ranch-style house on an oversize lot. She felt a bit nervous when she saw all the cars.

"I don't know if I can do this."

"Of course you can."

Kristi's stomach growled again, letting her know what her body wanted. "It's okay I'm here?"

"Absolutely. My mom's philosophy is the more the merrier. Half the neighborhood came by around noon for brunch. Now that it's after dinner, it's just the immediate family."

Mitch helped her out of the car. Kristi saw a few faces at the living-room window, but they quickly disappeared.

When they reached the porch, an older version of Mitch opened the front door. Mr. Robbins had a kind face. Kristi returned his smile as she stepped inside. Mitch was behind her, and he dropped a hand on her shoulder as his mother and a woman carrying a baby entered the room. His mother looked warm and friendly, but the woman with the child studied Kristi with a wariness she didn't attempt to hide.

"Mom, Dad, Maria, I want to introduce you to Kristi Jensen."

"Hi." Overcome with rare shyness, Kristi clammed up. It was one thing to pretend for her father, but this was Mitch's family. Even if she did have some growing feelings for Mitch, she probably shouldn't have come.

But it was too late—Mitch's petite mother encircled Kristi in a bear hug. "Welcome. I'm Sue Ellen. Maria told us you weren't feeling well and that's why Mitch ran out. I'm glad you're better."

Mitch took control. "We came from the hospital. The doctor checked her out and she's fine. Mom, is there anything left to eat? Kristi and I are starving."

"You poor dears. Of course we have plenty. Enough food to feed a small army. This way."

Kristi glanced back, but Mitch waved her onward and she followed his mother into the dining room. Most of the plates had been cleared away, but some loose silverware remained.

"You sit here." Sue Ellen pulled out the chair at the end of the table. "What can I get you? Water? Soda? Tea?"

"Water would be great if it's not too much trouble."

"None at all. It's nice to meet you after hearing about you for years."

Mitch was in the living room with Maria, and as he finished the conversation, he lifted the baby from his sister's arms and brought her with him.

"So who do you have here?" Kristi asked as Mitch sat beside her.

"This is my niece and goddaughter, Jane." Mitch lifted Jane's hand and leaned down to whisper in her ear. "Can you say hi to Kristi?" He waved Jane's hand. "Hi, Kristi."

Jane assessed Kristi with wide brown eyes, her mouth hidden behind a big butterfly-shaped pacifier.

"How old is she?"

"Seven months. She's pulling herself up and crawling everywhere. Maria and I both walked at ten months, and I think she's planning on taking after our side of the family."

"Maria's her mom, the one you were talking to."

"Yes. Her husband, Paul, is in the basement, probably playing pool. It's our family vice and he's undefeated."

Jane reached for the knife. "Nope. Not that one," Mitch told her, giving her a spoon instead. She pulled out the pacifier, dropped it on the table and mouthed the spoon.

"She loves spoons." Mitch bounced Jane on his knee and she giggled. "She's the first grandchild and spoiled rotten."

"Here, I'll take her." Sue Ellen entered with two plates of food. She set them down and reached for the baby. "Mitch, get Kristi some clean silverware so you two can eat."

"You have a nice family," Kristi said, studying her plate. Everything smelled delicious. She had lamb, couscous, green beans, glazed carrots and two rolls.

"Thanks." Mitch handed Kristi some flatware. Once seated, he lifted his fork. "Eat. If you play pool, maybe later you can try to defeat Paul."

"Not if he's as good as you say. But I can give it a shot. I used to play a little, and I don't think Dr. Krasnoff banned me. Is bending over okay?"

"I didn't see it on the list of things to avoid. As long as an activity is not strenuous and you aren't trying to touch your toes, you should be okay."

"I'd like to play."

Mitch's laugh was full and rich, and as always, it created a sense of warmth inside her. "Then you'll fit in. Around here, that's all it takes."

He wasn't kidding, Kristi discovered later. Once they were done eating, she and Mitch descended into the finished basement, where they found the rest of his family.

"My dad did all the work," Mitch said as Kristi

surveyed the rec room. The carpet was Berber, and neon beer signs and autographed sports memorabilia decorated the painted drywall. A working wet bar stood near the billiard table, and at the other end of the basement was a plasma TV and a sectional sofa.

Mitch introduced her to everyone, but as she'd met over ten people in less than thirty seconds, she was still connecting names with faces when Mitch placed a pool cue in her hand and told her they were playing Lauri and Cristos in the next round.

"The two getting married," Kristi remembered as she watched Lauri rack the balls. Like Mitch, Lauri had dark hair and eyes, same as her Greek fiancé.

Mitch moved to the end of the table, bent over and sent the cue ball flying. "We're stripes," he announced as one of the balls fell into a side pocket. He sank one more before missing and sending play over to the other team.

"You're not too bad," Kristi said as Mitch returned to her side.

"Those shots were luck," he claimed and they waited while Cristos scratched. "Better luck next time," Mitch told his future brother-in-law. Mitch pointed to the felt. "You're up."

"Okay." Kristi moved to the edge of the table and started assessing her shots. She'd learned the game from her dad, who had a room in their house devoted to a professional-grade table.

"Mitch, you did teach her how to play, didn't you?" Lauri teased. "And Kristi, even if you lose, you have to come to our engagement party. Has Mitch asked you yet?"

"No," Kristi said.

"Mitch, ask her," Lauri insisted.

"Let her shoot first," Mitch replied.

Kristi chalked the end of her cue. She eyed her shot, drew back and connected. The cue ball shot forward, hitting a solid with a resounding *thwack*. The solid and the cue ball then veered course, sending two striped balls falling into opposite corner pockets. Lauri and Cristos groaned.

"You've been hustled," Nick called out. Taller and broader than Mitch, he took a longneck beer out of the basement refrigerator and popped the top.

Mitch high-fived Kristi's outstretched hand. "Keep that up," he encouraged.

"I'll try." Kristi walked around the table, working out the angles and trajectories. She picked her shot, and sent the white ball down the entire length of the table. It connected with the edge of a stripe, sending the ball into a corner pocket.

"Mitch, you *are* hustling us," Lauri protested after Kristi sank yet another shot.

"One of us had to bring someone home who could beat Paul," Mitch said, giving Kristi another high five.

"Hey, I couldn't even play before I met your sister," Cristos protested.

"And we love you anyway," Amy teased. Her sister Melanie nodded.

"I don't have a good shot, so it'll be your turn." Kristi sent the cue ball to a corner.

Lauri walked around the table and pouted. "You didn't leave me one, either."

"That was the point," Mitch said. He was sitting on a bar stool, and he drew Kristi between his legs and against his chest as they watched Lauri figure out what she wanted to do. "You lied. You are good at this," he whispered in her ear.

Leaning on him was nice. "Maybe a little, but I don't like to brag," Kristi told him.

"Then I might have to keep you around. You're the best partner I've had."

"I'll be too fat to play soon."

He brushed her hair off her neck. "Never."

Lauri made one shot, but not the next. Kristi stepped out of Mitch's way and during his turn he went on to clear the table.

"Yes!" Kristi shouted as the eight ball fell, and they shared a celebratory hug.

"The table is under our control," Mitch called to the onlookers. "Who's next?"

"You might be unbeatable tonight. But we'll try." Logan, who was a younger version of Nick, grabbed a stick.

By the end of the evening, Kristi couldn't believe she'd had so much fun. She tried to remember the last time she'd laughed this much. Mitch's family was great company and so was he.

She hated to leave, but it was past ten and she had to

work tomorrow. "It was nice to meet all of you," Kristi called as they went up the stairs. They said goodbye to his parents and Mitch took her home.

"Glad you came?" Mitch asked as they drove.

She'd been afraid at first, but it had turned out better than she'd hoped. "Yes. You have a great family."

"Not too rowdy for you?"

"No."

After a brief lull in which the song on the radio changed, he said, "They liked you."

"Really? I wasn't sure. Your sister Maria…" Kristi paused, uncertain what to say.

"Maria doesn't like anyone. Just ignore her."

Kristi sensed there was more, but Mitch was turning onto her street. He walked her up to her door, and followed her when she invited him in. "All I have is soda and decaffeinated coffee."

"I'm good. I probably shouldn't stay."

"Thank you for today. For everything."

"I told you we're friends."

Suddenly she wanted their relationship to be more. She wished she could be that dream girl, and not just a fake date.

But before she could say anything, Mitch kissed the top of her forehead. "Sleep well, Kristi, and I'll see you tomorrow."

And with that, he was gone.

Chapter Eleven

"So tell me, where do we stand?" Larry Jensen glanced around the conference room. "Have you made any progress?"

Kristi watched as Mitch reached for his coffee. Since Easter, Mitch had been oddly distant. Sure, they'd put up a good front, but something had changed. Maybe it was the intensity of their jobs. They were down to the wire on contract talks. Whatever it was, she didn't like it.

"They still don't agree on the benefits plan," Mitch said, catching everyone's attention.

Larry frowned. "We need to get these negotiations finalized."

"I agree." Mitch took a sip and set his coffee aside. Down at the other end of the table, Marvin was nodding.

"Did you find any wiggle room?" Marvin asked.

"I think so."

Mitch pressed a key on his laptop, projecting a slide onto the conference room screen. The union negotiations were stalled, and the contract would expire in three days. Kristi's father had attended this meeting to personally assess the team's progress. She knew he was worried.

"Here's what I would suggest we do," Mitch said, starting his presentation.

Hours later, after a working lunch, those in the room had come to an agreement. They'd finished drafting a new proposal right around quitting time, and the dark mood had lifted. All around her, people were getting to their feet and exiting, ready to go home early for a change.

Kristi rested back against her chair, satisfied. The proposal was damn good; Mitch had found a way that the company could meet its growth targets and still satisfy key union demands. She'd send out a press release before she left this evening that Jensen was ready to propose a compromise.

She moved a hand to her stomach, feeling the little fluttering underneath her fingers. She'd started noticing fetal movement a few days ago, but hadn't realized at first what was going on. She'd read that first-time moms often missed the baby's kicking, not recognizing it as it wouldn't be more pronounced until the baby was a little bigger.

Mitch paused in packing away his laptop and leaned over. "Are you okay?"

"Baby's moving," she whispered.

A few heads turned their way, but most people had lost interest in the novelty of Mitch and Kristi being a couple. There'd been a lot of company watercooler gossip and speculation at first, but it had faded. She wasn't sure they'd managed to convince her father their relationship was real, but everyone else seemed to buy into it. The problem was, she had no idea how to end the charade and she wasn't sure she wanted to end it. Alison had been right—she was falling in love with Mitch.

As Kristi rose to her feet, one of the secretaries did a double take. "When are you due?"

Since she was forbidden to exercise or exert herself, Kristi's stomach had rounded outward with a vengeance. So far she'd kept the pregnancy quiet, but now the secret was out. "September."

"Congratulations. To you, too, Mitch."

"Uh," Mitch stammered, but the secretary was already breezing out.

Kristi placed her hand on the back of her chair. "Are you okay?" Mitch asked.

"Fine. Um, I have to go draft this press release. How about I call you later?"

Mitch frowned. "I thought we were meeting your parents at the club?"

"I'm going to cancel. I'm tired."

He was immediately concerned. "Get some rest. I'll drop by your office before you leave."

Ten minutes later, Alison entered Kristi's office. "You sounded upset when you phoned me a moment ago, so I got my mom to watch my kids in case you needed me. Do you want to go out to dinner?"

"No. I've lost my appetite." Kristi told her about the secretary's comment in the boardroom.

Alison whistled low. "I was worried about this."

"And you didn't say anything?"

"The doctor told you not to stress out. I figured why make you worry about the inevitable early? You know you'd obsess over it."

"So everyone thinks the baby is Mitch's?"

"It's better than them thinking it's Bill's."

"This is getting so out of control." Kristi banged her fist lightly on the chair arm. "He's going to suspect."

"As much as I hate to say this, you've got to tell him."

"I can't. He'll hate me for not telling him sooner. Besides, he likes someone else. How can I ruin his future?"

"So change it."

"What?"

"You're falling for him. Steal him away from that stupid dream girl. Make him fall in love with you. Then spring it on him. He'll be thrilled."

"Did your mother drop you on your head when you were a baby?"

"I'm serious. How else did you think this might end?"

"I don't know. Every move I make is the wrong one."

"Which is why you need to be honest. This has gone way too far. Your house of cards is built on lies. You're too involved. The truth always comes out, and you care for him. Tell him now."

Kristi's eyes widened. Mitch was coming down the hall. "He's here."

"Good luck. I'll talk to you later. If you need me I'll be at home." Alison rose, said hi to Mitch and left.

"Get everything done?" Mitch asked, giving her a smile that curled her toes.

"Yeah. I did." He came around the desk and began to massage her shoulders. His fingers were magic. "Mitch?"

"What?"

"I'm sorry I put you in this situation. I'm keeping you from having a real girlfriend. A real life. A real love. And everyone's going to assume you're the father of my child."

"I care about you. I told you that before. Let's not speculate on things that don't matter. I'm here because I want to be."

She let her head fall forward so he could better reach her neck. "Is your plan working?"

"What plan?"

"Making your dream girl jealous?"

"I'm starting to think that doesn't matter anymore. Kristi, I—"

His fingers kept working magic, but he'd stopped talking. "What?" she asked.

"Nothing."

"Maybe I should start. I think I want to make this real. Would you be willing to see if you and I could be more than friends?"

"What brought this on?"

"I think I'm developing feelings."

His fingers stilled and she froze, almost too fearful to move. She'd put herself out there. Then his fingers began to work again. "I'd like to make this real, too. You mean a lot to me," he said.

She didn't totally relax. "However, I am worried. I fail at relationships all the time. You and I could be ruining a good friendship."

"Or we could be making it better."

He spun her chair around so that she faced him. His eyes had darkened and he leaned down, capturing her lips with his. A shiver of pleasure ran through her and she sighed as he deepened the kiss. She threaded her hands into his dark hair, enjoying the silky texture, and lost herself in the moment.

When they finally broke apart, he smiled and gently wiped the corner of her lip with his thumb. "There."

"Wow."

"I'd say." He helped her to her feet and he arched an eyebrow, mirth crossing his face. "So my kisses are okay?"

She grinned. "They'll do."

"I'll have to work on that."

And as Mitch kissed her again, Kristi decided that this was definitely better than friendship.

KRISTI HAD NEVER been to a party in a church basement before she accompanied Mitch to Lauri and Cristos's engagement party that Friday. The place was packed.

Music blared from speakers attached to an iPod and

paper streamers reading Congratulations hung from the ceiling and walls. A table hosted a photo display of the engaged couple. Women were setting up a potluck on a long series of tables. Compared to catered events with their perfect silver buffet servers, the food tonight came in a plethora of mismatched disposable containers.

"Kristi!" Sue Ellen approached, her hands extended to envelop Kristi in a big hug. "I'm so glad you could make it. How's the baby doing?"

"Constantly kicking," Kristi replied.

"Let me feel." Sue Ellen placed her hands on Kristi's stomach. "The little tyke is active."

Mitch's mom straightened and turned to her son. Kristi indicated the outstretched plate Mitch held. "I made brownies."

"Her very first attempt," Mitch boasted. "I sampled them and they're good."

Kristi beamed under Mitch's praise. They were just a box mix, but she'd done it herself rather than stopping at a bakery.

"Mitch, put the food over there." Sue Ellen directed Mitch to a table covered with desserts. "You come with me." She took Kristi's arm and propelled her through the crowd. "There are people I want you to meet. That's Mitch's grandmother, my mother-in-law." Sue Ellen gave a small wave. "We'll talk to her later. My mom's first or she'll never speak to me again. She's been dying to meet you."

"So you're the girl who's snagged our Mitch," Mitch's

grandmother said in greeting. "He sure talks about you a lot."

"Thank you." As the evening wore on, Kristi relaxed. No one seemed to think it strange that Mitch was dating his pregnant former boss. Most accepted her easily, and Logan reminded her they had to play pool again.

By the time the buffet line started, she'd met almost every relative Mitch had. She'd even met his first girl-friend, a high school sweetheart who'd been a friend of Maria's. She was now married with three children and had wished Kristi well.

Once she and Mitch had filled their plates, they sat on metal folding chairs at one of several long tables placed end to end. Maria and Paul sat down across from them.

"Ready for that pool game?" Paul asked.

"Absolutely." Kristi reached for a fried chicken wing.

"Too bad there's no table here or we'd beat you tonight," Mitch added.

"As if," Paul said with a laugh.

"So, are enjoying yourself?" Maria asked as the guys began to talk pool.

Kristi nodded. "I am."

"Did Great-grandma Major ask when you and Mitch are getting married?"

"She did," Kristi admitted. Mitch's great-grand-mother had also crossed herself a few times when she'd seen Kristi's stomach. Kristi hadn't been certain if Great-grandma had been cursing her or praying for her.

"Don't worry. She's always like that." Lauri and Cristos sat down to Kristi's left.

Cristos used his fork to scoop up some baked beans. "Yeah, you should have heard her when we said we might hold our wedding at the botanical garden instead of a church. It's not like we wouldn't have a priest officiating."

"It wasn't pretty," Lauri added, dipping a carrot stick into some ranch dressing.

"So, have you decided on a venue?" Kristi asked, steering the conversation to safer waters.

"Not yet," Lauri admitted, and dinner continued.

Afterward, Kristi excused herself to use the restroom. Maria was waiting for her when she exited the stall.

"Hi."

"Hi." Kristi began to wash her hands.

Maria leaned her hip against one of the porcelain sinks and didn't mince words. "I figured we needed to talk."

"All right." Kristi reached for a towel. Of all the family members, Maria had been the least welcoming.

"What are you doing with Mitch?"

The rough brown paper crumpled between Kristi's hands. "Excuse me? We're dating."

"You aren't the type of girl who dates guys like my brother."

"I'm not following you." Actually, Kristi was, but

she really didn't want to get in a fight. Not tonight. Not when she and Mitch had just decided to make this real.

"You aren't from our world. Are you slumming?"

Kristi's denial came quick. "What? No!"

"Then what are your intentions? Everyone out there is asking Mitch when his own engagement's coming. I don't want you playing with my brother's heart, much less breaking it."

"Mitch and my relationship is our business."

Maria tilted her head. "True, but as you can tell from all the revelry out there, our family is extremely close. We know everyone's business. We also know Mitch has had a thing for you for years, and suddenly, here you are by his side."

"He's had a thing for me?"

Maria looked at Kristi as if she'd grown two heads. "Why do you think he kept working for you instead of taking a promotion? And all of a sudden, now that you need a father for your baby, you notice him. That's a little too convenient for my liking. It was bad enough when you were his boss. My brother's a good man. You have him wrapped around your finger and I don't like it."

Kristi bristled and squared her shoulders. "I care for Mitch. I don't intend to hurt him. You'll have to be satisfied with that. This is our business."

Maria frowned, not conceding. "I don't mean to be rude, but I want you to understand something. We've all been waiting for him to find a nice girl and settle down.

But ever since he started working for you, he can't keep a relationship."

Kristi's eyes narrowed and she remembered the dream girl, and Louisa, with whom he'd had no sparks. "You're saying I've been in the way of him finding happiness."

"You've been quite the diversion. You need something and he drops everything to come running. It's like he has blinders on where you're concerned, and what's worse is that you don't even see him for the wonderful guy he is. Until now, when you need him around to protect you."

"I don't need him to protect me."

"This isn't a joke to him. To him your relationship is very serious. He's wanted you for so long, and now here you are. His dream finally came true."

At those words, Kristi paled. Beside her, Maria immediately appeared worried. "Are you okay? I didn't mean to upset you by all this. I only wanted you to realize the truth. This isn't a game to my brother."

Maria was the least of Kristi's concerns. "I'm fine. I need to talk to Mitch."

Kristi left the bathroom. Mitch was on the dance floor, doing the electric slide with a group of relatives, including his great-grandmother. Seeing Kristi's face, he left the dance floor and came to put his arm around her shoulders, supporting her with his strength.

"What's wrong?" he asked. Maria had followed Kristi out. "Maria, if you—"

"I'm the dream girl who never noticed you."

Mitch frowned. "What?"

"The girl you told me about before the Christmas party. That was me. I thought all along she was someone else. I was jealous of myself."

How had her life gotten so crazy? She couldn't believe that. Mitch, who she'd considered a friend, had been hiding long-standing feelings from her.

"What was I supposed to say? You weren't interested in me. You were my boss. It was better to pretend."

"It's like being lied to."

"How? Okay, maybe I let you assume. But I wanted to be with you, and you would have run for the hills if you'd known how I felt. You asked for only one night."

Until she'd become pregnant, when she'd asked for more. Maria's words were like a fist of guilt squeezing Kristi's heart. "I want to leave. I don't feel well. Please take me home."

"Yeah, let's go." Mitch took his keys out of his pocket and led her to his car.

When they reached her house, Kristi hopped out before he could come around and open her door. He caught up with her as she fumbled for her house keys. "Kristi…"

She turned to him. "I want to be alone tonight. If you care for me like you say you do, you'll let me be and give me time to think this over. Please go home."

Mitch backed off. She could tell she'd hurt him by the pain in his eyes. "I don't understand, but okay."

She pulled her door open, relieved when he didn't try

to stop her. Soon she was inside, and moments later she heard his car drive away.

"I CAN'T BELIEVE he's liked you all this time." Alison lifted the coffee mug to her lips. In response to Kristi's text message, she'd brought half a dozen freshly baked doughnuts over first thing Saturday morning, and Kristi had poured out the entire story.

"I can't believe I missed the signs, either. How could I be so blind?"

Kristi folded her legs underneath her. She'd turned on the air conditioner, and her feet were cold. The baby moved, and she reached for another doughnut, this one chocolate with chocolate icing and filling. "I guess the good thing about being pregnant is that all this stress eating doesn't count."

"You can pig out and eat whatever you want. It's a wonderful nine months," Alison agreed.

Kristi bit down to get both pastry and fluffy chocolate filling. She savored it for a few seconds before speaking. "I am so confused. I don't get it. If he liked me, why didn't he ask me out? Especially after we made love. Why all this silly subterfuge?"

Alison shook her head. "I don't know. Like he said, you told him one night. He was respecting your wishes."

"And what guy does that?"

"Mitch." Alison grabbed another doughnut.

"Just when I thought things couldn't get more complicated. We'd just decided not to pretend."

"And we see how well that worked out. You decide to fake date Mitch, and it becomes real. Your dad wants you married so badly he's probably counting down the days until you fall for Mitch. No wonder he called your bluff."

So that was why he'd been so smug lately. He wanted her to marry Mitch. Kristi hadn't gotten her father's reaction quite right. He didn't want her to be a single mother. Under these circumstances, Mitch would seem perfectly suitable for his daughter. She sighed and ate the last of her doughnut. She reached for the third pastry. "So where do I go from here?"

"You tell Mitch the truth about how you feel and about the baby. You wouldn't be getting in the way of true love. Heck, you *are* his true love."

"Which means he'll be all over me trying to do the right thing."

"Is that really so bad? It's the solution to all your problems."

Kristi sat back with a thump, powdered sugar coating her fingers. "Why didn't you warn me sparks caused so much trouble?"

Alison shrugged. "I thought I did, and I sure didn't know you'd sleep with Mitch."

Kristi ate some of her third doughnut, trying to think. But no answers came. "Tell me, is it irrational that I'm upset? Is this all hormonal? It's like I'm on a roller coaster and I can't get off."

"You're going to have a baby. That changes everything."

Kristi couldn't shake the black cloud hanging overhead. "I've made a big mess and it's getting worse."

"You have a hunky man who worships you and treats you like a queen. I'd kill for that. Kristi, be honest. How do you feel about Mitch?"

"Guilty. I asked him to sleep with me because I wanted to feel desirable. I can't believe I didn't realize he had a crush on me. Why can't I pick someone up and have it be simple?"

"Do you like Mitch?"

"Yes." She could say that easily.

"Do you love Mitch?"

"I don't even know what love is. Is it what I felt for Bobby Jones our sophomore year, until he dumped me for Marla Evans? Is it what I thought I felt for Bill? How do I know when I've met Mr. Right? And how do I share my life?"

"You just do."

"What if I fail? I've screwed up every other time."

Alison shrugged. "It's the risk you take. But you have to start by being honest with yourself. You like spending time with Mitch and he makes your pulse race. Why is that? Figure out how you really feel and tell Mitch the truth. Even if that means spilling all your secrets."

"I'm not very good at that."

Alison snagged the last doughnut. "Then, my friend, you're going to have to learn."

Chapter Twelve

By Monday morning Mitch still hadn't spoken with Kristi. He'd heard from her, if one measly text message saying she'd see him at the office counted.

He had a meeting with Larry, so he headed for the CEO's office just before 10:00 a.m. After a five-minute wait, the secretary sent him in. "Have we heard back from the union?" Mitch asked as Larry waved him forward.

"That'll probably be tomorrow. They have to vote. Sit down." Mitch sat across Larry's desk. "So how was your sister's engagement party?"

Mitch had no idea what Kristi had told her parents. "We had a nice time."

"Good. I thought it might be difficult for Kristi, what with another person getting married before her."

That hadn't been what had upset her. "I don't think your daughter is really all that focused on marriage."

"Of course she is. All women are, whether they'll admit it or not. Kristi's sidetracked by the fact that she's pregnant, that's all. I think the right man could convince her quite quickly."

"Are you saying that I'm that guy?"

"I'm asking your intentions toward her, yes. You'll be headed back to your division, Kristi to hers. The job of getting her to stay home hasn't been accomplished."

"She has balanced work and pregnancy just fine."

"Did your mother stay home?"

Mitch nodded. "She did."

Larry leaned back as if that proved his point. "How much do you like my daughter?"

"Sir?"

"It's a simple question. You two are dating."

"Yes."

"So it's not a smoke screen after all."

"It's never been that on my end."

Larry seemed pleased. "I didn't think so. Where do you see this relationship heading? Speak to me as her father, not as your boss."

Mitch knew nothing but total honesty would do. "I care about her a great deal. I love her, but I'm not sure my feelings are returned."

"That's fixable," Larry declared.

"I'm not about to go all underhand. I want her to love me for who I am. That takes time."

"You don't have time. There's a baby on the way. Mitch, you weren't what I envisioned for my son-in-law, but you love her, and you're a good man."

"I've loved her for a long time," Mitch admitted.

"I wondered. Well, if that's the case, do something about it. Win her over."

"I plan to try."

"Good. So let me help. I'm sending you back to the Communications Department. While I won't promote you to vice president until after you're married, I will put you second in command."

"That's Brett's job."

"I'm sending him to Distribution."

"I really don't think this is a good idea right now."

"Of course it is. You two need to spend time together. Mitch, this is an opportunity of a lifetime. I'd think it over carefully."

Mitch got to his feet. "Believe me, I will."

BY TWO, when Kristi caught up with her father, her nerves were shot. She'd asked Mitch for space, and as he had after the Christmas party, he'd given it to her. He hadn't even answered her text message.

"You look tired," her dad remarked as she stepped into his office.

"I'm fine," she replied automatically. No need for her dad to worry. He was already trying to push her out.

"Well, hopefully I have some good news. I'm transferring Mitch back to your department and sending Brett to Distribution."

"Why?"

"You and Mitch work well together—you two are quite the pair. And he's much better suited there than where he is. This was a business decision."

"You never say that unless it isn't."

"He's the only person you'll trust with your job when you're on maternity leave. I'm thinking long-term here.

You are having a baby, and you will not work from home. Maternity leave is just that, leave. Don't take this personally."

Her father reached for a pen and twirled it. "Mitch is the best candidate. All I want is what's best for you and for Jensen."

"You just want me married."

"I admit I dropped a few hints Mitch's way. I'm an old man. I get to do those things. It's obvious you care for Mitch. He was the first one you called Easter weekend when you were having complications."

Kristi could be as stubborn as her dad. "I could have driven to the hospital myself."

"But you didn't," Larry pointed out. "You wanted him there."

She had.

"I'd even venture that you have deep feelings for him."

"Maybe." She'd realized that this weekend during all her soul-searching. Besides Alison, he'd become her best friend. She didn't want to lose him.

Her father studied her for a moment "Mitch cares for you more than you realize. Think about how many opportunities he passed up so he could continue to work with you."

"I'm surprised you didn't fire him for staying close."

"Why would I?"

"You had Randy fired and he didn't even work here."

"That was different. I've mellowed. As for Mitch, I like him."

"You and Mom are constantly fixing me up with guys from a certain social class."

"Well, those are the only people we know."

Figuring out her life was like putting together a thousand-piece all-white puzzle—next to impossible. "This is crazy."

"What? That you found someone you like and he likes you back? I'd say it's about damn time. Don't mess this one up."

"Dad...I'm scared."

Larry leaned down to give her a hug. "I know, sweetheart. I know."

"What am I going to do?"

"You'll figure it out. You always do."

"That doesn't help."

Larry released her. "You've got a great man there. Maybe you should tell him how you feel."

Larry rested his fingers on the door frame. "You know I love you. Your mother and I both do. Now, I'm late for a meeting, but feel free to stay as long as you like."

Kristi leaned back against the chair. She did trust Mitch with her department. She was pretty sure he'd do the right thing and step aside when she returned—he was an honorable guy. She needed to see him. She rose, used her father's private bathroom to freshen up and took the elevator to Mitch's floor.

"I'm sorry, Ms. Jensen, he's left for the day," Mitch's secretary told her.

"But it's only two."

"He left after lunch. Said he was going home," she replied.

Back in her office, Kristi dialed Mitch's number, but it went straight to voice mail.

Well, they needed to talk. Grabbing her purse, she headed for her car.

AFTER THREE MINUTES of ringing Mitch's doorbell, Kristi decided that maybe she'd made a dumb move. He obviously wasn't home.

She went back down the walkway, toward the street, but paused as a whirring sound came from the backyard. She listened for a moment, and then walked around the side of the house and through the gate. The yard was empty, but a door into the garage was open and as she walked toward it, the noise became louder.

She poked her head inside. The two-car garage didn't house any autos. Instead, it was filled with machinery. Mitch was cutting wood with a table saw. He finished the piece and then, as if sensing someone, glanced up. He turned off the machine and removed his safety goggles.

"Hi."

"Hi," Kristi answered, stepping inside. Mitch had all the doors open, but despite the ventilation, the garage smelled of wood stain and sawdust. The aroma wasn't wholly unpleasant. "I didn't know you did this."

"Yeah. It's a hobby of mine. Got it from my dad."

"So you build things."

"Tables. Chairs. Beds. Furniture mostly, but I also like to carve. I made my mom a nativity set for Christmas."

"I admit, I'm impressed."

"It's nothing, really."

"You cook and make furniture. I'd say you're pretty amazing."

"Keep complimenting me and it'll go to my head." He wiped his hands on his jeans and grabbed something off a workbench. "Here."

He handed her a small object, a bluebird of happiness about the size of a baseball. The bluebird statue was usually made of glass, and it was always given to wish someone peace and joy. Mitch had made this one out of wood.

The blue-stained oak was smooth to the touch, and she ran her fingers over the piece. "It's beautiful."

"Keep it."

"Really?"

His face remained impassive. "Yes. I made it for you a few days ago because you seemed unhappy. I'd hoped it might make you smile. It's finally finished."

"I'm sorry I've been such a nightmare."

"You haven't. You've been overwhelmed. I understand."

"My dad told me he's moving you back to the Communications Department."

"Yeah. I found out this morning."

"Which is why you left?"

"I'm not sure it's a good idea. You need space. Having me underfoot is not going to give you that."

"You can't quit."

The corner of his lips inched upward. "No. I won't. But I'll need to finagle your dad into putting me back where I was."

"He's stubborn."

"So are you."

She sighed and set the bird down. "I have no idea what to do anymore."

"Whatever you do, don't put any of the blame on yourself. You don't need any additional stressors and I went into our relationship with my eyes wide-open. Getting to date you, making love with you, it was wonderful. It was what I'd always wanted."

"You sound like you're breaking up with me."

"I don't know what we are."

"Are we fighting? If so, it's unlike any fight I've ever had."

"Maybe it's a chance for us to be totally honest. Clear the air. Bare it all. If that doesn't work, I'll refuse the transfer, and you and I can go back to being on different floors and never seeing each other."

"I don't think I'd like that."

"But it's our out."

Panic clutched at her, and she rubbed her throat. "I don't want out."

His eyebrow arched and he folded his arms across his T-shirt. "No?"

"No. But I'm scared. You have all these feelings you never shared. Everything seems so overwhelming..."

"You said be honest, so here it is. From the first moment I set eyes on you, I wanted you like I'd never wanted anyone before. All the girls I tried to date paled next to you. When we made love, it was like discovering nirvana. Walking away from you the next morning was horrible. I wanted to stay."

"Then why didn't you?"

"Because you asked me to go. You only wanted one night. So I went and didn't contact you. And I'll go again if that's what you want."

"I don't." Of that she was certain. She stared at the bird. He'd made it with his own hands. Hands that had caressed her body and loved her well. He'd given her the life growing inside her.

"I could make you happy. I feel complete when I'm with you. You're my soul mate, Kristi," he said.

"Do those really exist?"

His smile was sad. "I believe so. All those failed relationships have made you cynical."

"So even now, after everything we've been through—"

"I'm more positive than ever that you're exactly what I want for the rest of my life. I trust my gut. I always have."

"No one's ever said these things to me before."

"That's because none of the men you've dated have been right for you."

A bold assertion.

"Ask me," he said.

"Ask you what?"

"Ask me what you really want to know." He stood there, quietly waiting. She'd done this before. Said the words. Asked the loaded, life-altering question that usually led to her breakups.

Her mouth suddenly felt dry, and she had to force her tongue to move. "Do you love me?"

His eyes never left her face. "Yes."

One word, but that *yes* had Kristi inhaling several deep breaths. How many times had she told someone she'd loved them, only to be met with stony silence?

But Mitch loved her. He hadn't hesitated. Not once.

"It's okay if you can't say the words back," Mitch told her. "I don't expect you to have those feelings yet. Not when we haven't been truly honest until now. What you give me is enough. What we've shared lately is more than I'd dreamed."

"Sparks."

He frowned. "What do those have to do with anything?"

She straightened. "Sparks. Passion. We have that."

"We do. But we have much more than that. We're friends. We care about each other. We get along and enjoy each other's company. My feelings run deep. I love you."

"You won't after you hear what I have to say."

"We're being honest. Whatever you have to say, I can handle."

She bit her lip, and then blurted it out before fear paralyzed her. "The baby is yours."

Chapter Thirteen

Ten seconds was long enough to make a touchdown pass. Thirty seconds was long enough to make a sane woman crazy. The dust-covered clock flickered, indicating two minutes had passed. The silence was deafening.

Mitch hadn't even looked at her. After her announcement, he'd picked up some sandpaper and begun to run it over a piece of wood about the size of a cable-box remote control. He'd tuned her out.

Kristi couldn't take it anymore. "Mitch, please, talk to me."

"What do you want me to say?" He lifted his head, letting her see his face. The pain in his eyes stabbed her like a knife. "What am I supposed to say? All this time you've known I'm the father and you let me think it was someone else's baby. How should I respond to that?"

"I don't know. Yell. Curse. Tell me I'm despicable. Do something, but please don't shut me out."

He shook his head. "I'm holding on to my anger by a thread. And I'm still trying to absorb this. You told me you were safe."

"I thought I was. I was on the pill. The doctor thinks it's because I was taking antibiotics the week before we made love."

He turned the wood over and over in his hand. "So you're sure it's not Bill's."

"There's no way. I had a cycle in between. We hadn't been sleeping together toward the end. I didn't mean to get pregnant. It was an accident."

"And was it an accident that you forgot to tell me? How convenient." He crushed the sandpaper and tossed it onto the workbench. "I deserved to know. I went to the hospital with you! You could have been losing my baby!"

She didn't know what to say. He was right on all counts. Invoking the "it's my body" defense would be rude and insulting. "I had my reasons."

"It doesn't matter what your reasons were. It's my child and I should have been involved."

"I'm not having my baby live half the time with you and half with me." She covered her stomach protectively.

"Did I even suggest that? Already you're on the defensive. I'm the one who's been wronged here. You lied to me."

"I thought I was protecting you, saving you from an obligation you didn't want. I had no idea how you felt about me—you lied, too."

Mitch put the block down and flexed his hands, stretching the fingertips upward and out. "I don't think we should talk about this any further. Not now. I need to be alone."

"Mitch…"

"Please go. Let me think. I gave you space this weekend. Do me the same courtesy."

She stood there, aware that his anger was tightly contained. He turned his back on her. "I know where to find you," he said.

She didn't like walking away, but she had dropped a bombshell. He deserved to be mad and she couldn't fault him for wanting time. She would, too, under the circumstances. She climbed into her car, sat for a moment, then turned the key and drove away.

MITCH STOOD in his shop another five minutes before he closed the garage doors and crossed the backyard to his house. He washed his hands, dried them and then sat down in front of his plasma screen, all on autopilot.

Kristi Jensen was having his baby.

He'd been the biggest fool on the planet. How could he not have seen this? When she'd turned up pregnant, he'd just assumed it was Bill's. He should have asked. Should have at least suspected there might be a chance the baby was his.

At least then he wouldn't have been such a patsy, helping her out, pretending to date her, making it real, all while she was keeping a huge, life-altering secret from him. He was going to be a dad.

Hell. What a mess. This certainly wasn't how he'd expected to become a father. He'd figured he'd be married a few years and then he and his wife would decide to start a family.

Surprises sucked. He wasn't married, he was sort of dating Kristi—whose motivations for making things real he now questioned.

His cell phone rang, and seeing Maria's number, he flipped the phone open. "You have impeccable timing," he said without preamble.

"I called you at work to invite you to dinner this weekend and they said you'd left early. You never do that. Are you sick?"

Maria had always been astute, and she'd given him the perfect excuse. He could tell her that he'd gotten the flu. But that would be another lie. He was tired of lies.

"I found out today I'm going to be a father."

He heard her quick intake of breath. "Say what?"

"I'm the father of Kristi's child. Surprise."

"Holy Mary, mother of…" Maria's voice drifted away and there was silence before she said, "Well, we obviously know when the happy event took place. But she's just telling you now?" Her tone contained the same raw indignation that Mitch felt.

"My thoughts exactly. She dropped the truth on me today. Less than twenty minutes ago, in fact."

"This is a shock."

"Tell me about it." Mitch rummaged in his refrigerator for a cola. He popped the top on the aluminum can and took a long swallow. "I thought it was someone else's. How much of an idiot am I? It didn't even occur to me that the baby could be mine. I figured she'd tell me if it was, not wait until now. Not play all these games…"

"I told you not to lust after her in the first place. Play with fire and you get burned."

"Thanks for the twenty-twenty hindsight. It's quite helpful."

"So what are you going to do?"

"I'm not going to step aside. I want to be involved in my child's life."

"Which is probably why she didn't tell you." Maria whistled low. "But she can't deny you access to your child. The law won't let her."

Mitch leaned his hip against the counter. "While that's good to know, I'm hoping it won't come to that."

"Mitch, whatever you do, you have to protect yourself. She's only been with you because you're convenient, not because she really loves you. You need to get yourself a lawyer before you talk to her again."

"That's a little too mercenary for me. I know you're only trying to protect me, but I'll handle it. If I need legal counsel, I'll get some."

"Of course I'm worried."

"And I love you for it. But I also love Kristi."

"How can you?"

"Well, I'm furious, but my feelings haven't changed. I don't hate her. I understand how she thinks. Her father's been after her to quit working from the moment she told him she was expecting, and she probably didn't want yet another man trying to influence her decisions. She also may have been trying to protect me."

"I don't see how that's possible."

"If Larry Jensen knew I'd slept with his daughter he would fire me and make me so unhirable in this town that I'd need to move to find a job." As Mitch talked to his sister, he began to see the bigger picture.

Kristi was just as confused as he was. Twenty years of dating failures had broken her heart. She was afraid to trust again.

"Are you there?" Maria asked.

"Yeah. Sorry. I was thinking. Maybe this is what Kristi and I need to bring us together."

"You cannot be serious."

"I am. I know you aren't her biggest fan and this is another big black mark against her, but she cares for me. I know she does. And all the secrets between us are gone."

Calm overtook him, replacing the anger. He had to believe Kristi had come to him because she'd decided over the weekend that she wanted to work things out. They'd had a lot of issues to wade through. Maybe it was time to strip everything bare and start over with nothing between them.

"I'll talk to you later," he told his sister, hanging up.

ALISON HAD ANSWERED Kristi's call on the first ring. She'd listened to everything Kristi had told her and made the appropriate noises. "So what am I going to do?" Kristi asked.

"You could just marry him."

That had Kristi's attention. "What?"

"Marry him. Your dad likes Mitch. He's the baby's father…"

"Hold up." Kristi stood and started pacing her kitchen floor. "I do not want to get married. We just made this dating thing real."

"Maybe you'll have to skip the appetizer and go straight to the main course. You've already sampled the dessert."

Trust Alison to put things in such crass perspective. "This wasn't supposed to happen."

"Kristi, no bad things in life are supposed to happen but they do. Mitch is the father. Marriage signifies commitment. He's a good man. He's crazy about you. Heck, you're the girl of his dreams."

"What about what I want?"

"Do you even know what that is?" Alison asked the question Kristi had been wrestling with.

"Yes. Love. Passion. Affection. Happily ever after…" Kristi's doorbell rang. "Someone's at the door." She went to peer out the window. "It's Mitch."

"Then talk to him." And with that, Alison hung up.

MITCH CLUTCHED the bouquet of roses in his left hand and rang Kristi's doorbell again. His stomach churned and he rolled his shoulders, trying to ease the tension consuming him. He had no idea how this was going to play out.

When she opened the door he noticed she'd changed into lime-green maternity yoga clothes that hugged her belly. Inside that bulge his child grew.

"Hi," Mitch said, placing the dozen red roses in her hands. "I'm sorry for my reaction earlier."

Kristi stepped aside and let him in. "Thank you. These are beautiful."

She closed the door and he followed her to the kitchen where she sniffed the flowers before retrieving a vase. "I haven't had flowers in a while."

"Well, I aim to fix that."

Her eyes widened, and she stopped unwrapping the cellophane from the roses. "What do you mean?"

He took a deep breath. "Kristi, I want you in my life. To say that I'm shocked by this turn of events is an understatement. But that doesn't change how I feel. I'm angry, yes, but I still love you. I don't think I could ever stop loving you."

Her lips trembled. He reached for her hands. "Both of us have come clean. We've stripped our souls bare. Maybe that's what we needed. A fresh start."

"You still want to be with me?"

"Why wouldn't I? You're wonderful and sweet. You have passion and drive. I've always admired you."

"I'm your dream girl," she said quietly, looking down at her swollen belly.

"You aren't a dream girl. You're real. You're right here in front of me." He let go of one hand to touch her cheek. "I can only pray that someday you'll return my feelings."

"I don't know. That's what overwhelmed me this weekend when your sister told me. I'm not even sure what love really is."

"You will be when you feel it."

"And what if I'm not? How can you stay with me when I don't even know my own heart?"

"I'm willing to risk it. You and I are good together. I care for you, and—"

"I do care for you," she inserted.

"I know you do. Which is why I think we keep going the way we are. Dating. Feeling each other out. Doing what comes naturally."

She frowned. "You don't want to marry me?"

He smiled reassuringly. "I do. But not because you're having a baby. Not because you feel pressured to do something you don't want. I want you with me when you're ready."

She broke into fresh tears and he cradled her in his arms. "Shh. It's all going to be okay."

"You're too good for me."

"Maybe," he admitted with a grin, "but then I think you're too good for me."

"Your sister hates me. So will your parents."

"They'll all get over it. The only thing that matters is that I'm happy. And when I'm with you, I am."

He drew her closer and planted a kiss on her forehead. Her skin was soft beneath his lips. "I think we've survived our first two fights."

"Incredible."

"Yeah, it is. See? It's all going to be fine."

KRISTI HOPED he was right. She'd been in volatile relationships, once in her early twenties, staying longer than she should before wising up and calling things off. This fight hadn't been like that. They'd been mad at each other, but the anger had been diffused. They'd worked through things and at least come to a point where they'd found common ground.

He loved her. His words had made her all warm and fuzzy. He'd understood that she needed time. He was a special man.

She was connected to him in ways that she'd never been with anyone else. And she was having his child. They'd be forever linked because they'd created a life.

The baby kicked, and Mitch's hand dropped to her stomach. "Wow."

"He or she does that a lot."

The baby shifted, and then all was still. "Probably going to sleep," Mitch observed.

A lump formed in Kristi's throat. Mitch would make a great father. "Kiss me."

Mitch gazed into her eyes, uncertain he'd heard her correctly. "What?"

"Kiss me. Make me feel sparks. Show me that somehow we're going to be okay."

Mitch touched her face before kissing her gently. Heat pooled low.

"I'm not fragile." She moved his hands to her breasts. She needed him. "Touch me."

"They're bigger." His voice grew husky.

"More sensitive, too." She put her hands in his hair and lowered his head so she could kiss him more thoroughly.

"The doctor said—" Mitch began, but Kristi led him to the bedroom.

"There are other things we can do," she said. Mitch's only answer was a pleasurable groan.

"Stay the night," she asked much later, after they'd gotten up and had dinner. "Sleep with me."

"Okay," he agreed.

He curled her to him, and Kristi listened as his breathing became slow and regular. She felt safe and secure in his arms. "You'd never hurt me," she stated.

He stirred. "Not intentionally."

Her baby kicked, as if recognizing his father's voice. The jab pushed against Kristi's stomach, directly under where she'd placed her hand. It was as if the baby was saying, "Come on, Mom, get a clue."

Tears formed in her eyes and she asked another question. "Do you think how you feel could be enough for both of us?"

Mitch propped himself up on his elbow so he could face her. "I do."

She placed her hand on his cheek. The baby moved again.

"I saw that," Mitch marveled.

"He or she's awake," Kristi said.

He was fascinated with watching her stomach. "Amazing that this is mine."

"I'm sorry I didn't tell you."

"I'm sorry I was such a jerk earlier today."

His apology touched her, and called forth something from deep inside. "I do want you involved. Don't leave me."

"I won't. I can stay. We can continue this until you're ready to stop. Then we'll make arrangements."

That wasn't what she meant. "No. I mean promise me that no matter what happens down the road, you won't leave me. Everyone does."

"We're friends. I'll always be here."

"I want more than just friendship." As she said the words she realized she'd never been more certain of anything in her life. He covered the hand on his cheek with one of his own. "Mitch Robbins, will you marry me?"

Chapter Fourteen

Mitch stroked her hand tenderly. "You aren't ready. You're saying things in the heat of the moment."

Kristi had put herself out there and she bristled. "That's a lie and we said no more of those. I know what I want and I know exactly what marriage entails."

"I do want to marry you."

"Then why haven't you said yes?"

"Because you've changed your mind so quickly. You weren't certain what you wanted a few hours ago. What if your dream guy's waiting just around the corner?"

"He's not there. Tonight I realized that my dream guy's been right in front of me all along."

"Are you sure?"

"I am."

"Then yes. I would love to marry you." As Mitch said those words and sealed his fate, the weight of the world lifted from his shoulders. Things between them were going to be okay. "I'll make you happy," he promised.

"I believe you." Tears shone in her blue eyes, and he wiped one away before leaning over to kiss her. His sweet kiss morphed into a dedicated plunder of her mouth.

"Where do we go from here?" Kristi asked once they'd finally come up for air.

"We sleep."

"And then tomorrow?"

He heard her hesitancy. She wondered if he'd back out. "We'll discuss all the important details. A ring. An engagement announcement. A wedding. The future. We're in this together. You, me and baby."

"I promise I'll try to make you happy, too. At least I can give you companionship."

She'd already given him a lot more—she'd given him hope.

For Mitch had discovered something tonight. He dropped a kiss to her lips, which she eagerly returned. Kristi Jensen truly did love him. She just didn't realize it yet.

THEY WERE MARRIED in July, the earliest Emma Jensen and Sue Ellen Robbins could get an acceptable wedding ceremony together. Kristi had been fine with something simple in the courthouse, but had given in to the wishes of both sets of parents, who really wanted some sort of cleric officiating.

She and Mitch chose to have the ceremony and the reception at the Jensen estate. And Mitch's family priest, after rushing the required marriage classes, had performed the nuptials in Emma's rose garden.

Even Mother Nature had cooperated, providing a perfect day.

"You seem happy," Alison said later, coming into Kristi's childhood bedroom so she could help Kristi change into traveling clothes. Kristi's parents had given her and Mitch an Alaskan cruise for their honeymoon, and the charter jet would depart for Vancouver once Kristi and Mitch arrived at the airport.

"I am happy," Kristi replied, shedding the white tulle headpiece and matching silk, knee-length dress. A thin gold band had joined the diamond solitaire she'd been wearing on her left hand for weeks. "I still don't believe I'm married."

"He's a good man."

"He is." Kristi laid the dress on the bed. "Thank you for being here," she told Alison.

Alison wore the sleeveless sheath designating her maid of honor and only bridesmaid. "I wouldn't be anywhere else."

Kristi held up her hand, admiring the beautiful diamond, which reflected the early-evening sunlight. Up until the "I do's," she'd been afraid the wedding wouldn't occur.

She'd known her fear was irrational, but her boy-friend history had had Kristi holding her breath and praying Mitch wouldn't wake up one morning and say he'd made a mistake.

AFTER THEIR RETURN from their honeymoon, they'd settled into married life. Now, two weeks before her due date, Mitch had become an essential part of Kristi's world and she couldn't imagine herself without him.

They'd decided to live in her condo, since her place was bigger and closer to work. Mitch had been getting his house ready to go on the market. He'd catered to her late-night cravings, including many a midnight run to Dierberg's for apple pie and whipped cream.

He'd even painted the nursery. The only thing missing was the furniture. They planned to go shopping next week, after they saw what Kristi got at today's baby shower.

She unwrapped the next present, a silver piggy bank from one of her mother's friends. Emma's entire social set was in attendance, and the event was so large they'd held it at the country club.

"Thank you. This is wonderful." Kristi passed the gift to Alison, who recorded the item and giver before passing the piggy bank around for everyone's inspection.

"You're all so kind," Kristi said when she'd unwrapped everything. She was a bit overwhelmed by the generosity her family and friends had shown. She had almost everything she needed for the baby, including car seats, swings, strollers, savings bonds and clothes.

"There's one more gift," Sue Ellen said. Mitch's mother got to her feet. As if that was some sort of signal, a banquet attendant rounded a corner and entered the room, pushing a crib.

Kristi put her hand over her mouth. The wood was a dark cherry and the little mattress was made up with the comforter set she'd told Mitch she'd almost bought a few weeks ago. She could hear the murmurs of approval from the crowd.

"I was just telling Mitch we needed to get a crib and he told me not to worry. We plan to use a Moses basket for the first month, but…" Kristi stopped babbling.

The crib was perfect, the exact shade she'd told Mitch she wanted when they'd visited a baby furniture store. The attendant rolled the crib closer.

Sue Ellen's excitement bubbled out. "There's also a changer, but we didn't bring that. This is from our family to yours. It's become a tradition. When Maria was pregnant, Mike and Mitch made her crib. Mitch made this one for you all by himself. Mike and I bought the bunting. It's the one you liked, right?"

"Yes." Kristi had gotten to her feet and Alison put a steadying hand on the small of her back. She'd seen random pieces in Mitch's shop, but hadn't realized what he was building. And lately, when he'd been gone…

"I thought he was spending all those hours getting his house ready to sell."

Sue Ellen gave her a hug. "He couldn't move his wood shop until this was done."

"It's beautiful," someone said.

Sue Ellen beamed with pride. "It's solid cherry, hand-sanded and stained. Mitch cut every piece himself."

Kristi's guests had risen to their feet and were surrounding the crib. "That must have taken him forever," someone said.

"He started in April, after Easter. He worked on it mainly on the weekends and at night."

Kristi looked at Alison. Alison mouthed one word. "April."

He'd begun a crib, risking her rejection and the demise of their relationship. He'd done nothing but give. Even after she'd told him about the baby. How had she gotten so lucky?

"Are you going to touch it?" Sue Ellen asked. "Let me show you how it works."

The crowd parted so Kristi could see. "Did Mitch make the changer, too?" she asked.

"No. My husband did that. Mitch can't have all the fun."

Kristi ran her fingers over the railing, feeling the perfection of the smooth varnish. Not one bump marred the finish. "He did a beautiful job. He gave me a wooden bird once, but I never expected he could do this."

"Mitch is good at surprises. Oh, cake's here. Come on, everyone. Cake." Sue Ellen clapped her hands and soon the guests began to disperse back toward the tables where they'd eaten lunch.

"That's quite a gift," her mother said. Next to her, Alison nodded.

"Did you know?" Kristi asked.

Her mom nodded. "I saw it earlier. Sue Ellen had to show someone, she was so excited. I'd better go help her."

Despite their different social backgrounds, Sue

Ellen had won Emma over and the two had become fast friends. They'd even planned the shower together.

"If I didn't love you, I think I'd hate you," Alison said once everyone had moved out of earshot. She set her hand on the crib. "If you ever want to trade places, you just let me know."

"What, you'd take this basketball in my stomach?" she joked.

"No, your husband. Kristi, this crib is incredible."

Kristi hadn't yet lost the giddy feeling. "Isn't it? I wake up every morning and realize how lucky I am. He's so wonderful. This…" Kristi patted the crib, the joy she felt robbing her of words.

Alison shook her head and reached out to touch Kristi's hand. "Admit it, you love him."

"I…" Kristi's eyes widened and she gripped the side of the crib for support. "I do, don't I?"

Alison's smile was gentle and knowing. "I'd say you have for a while, but you didn't realize it."

"Wow."

"Yeah. Can you believe it? You have finally fallen head over heels with a man who loves you back."

"Kristi, time for a picture." Her mother waved at her to approach the custom-made cake shaped like a baby rattle.

"Coming."

"Duty calls," Alison said as she followed Kristi. "And don't worry. You're fine. No tears. You can do it. Smile."

"Thanks." Kristi's knees wobbled a little, but she

found her footing. She'd talk to Mitch once her shower ended. Confess everything. Tell him how she felt. Tell him that she loved him....

"SO HOW DO YOU THINK the ladies are doing?" Larry asked as he lined up his putt on the eighteenth hole.

Mitch checked his watch. While the girls-only baby shower had been going on, he and Larry had hit the links. "They're probably about finished. The shower's supposed to end around three."

"Never did understand the point of oohing and aahing over a bunch of baby stuff, but I guess that's because we're men." Larry sank the putt, retrieved his ball and marked down his score. "You're up."

Mitch didn't have as good a shot. He had to chip onto the green, and ended the hole two over par.

"Not too shabby," Larry said as he totaled Mitch's score. "You're definitely improving. I only beat you by ten."

"I've been practicing."

"That's what I like to hear. Let's go have a celebratory drink. I'm ready for one." Larry patted Mitch on the shoulder as they headed toward the clubhouse, leaving storing the clubs and returning the cart to the caddies they'd hired.

They entered the bar, chose seats in a booth and ordered. "I'm sure they'll find us in here when they're ready. That crib you made was pretty nice." Larry accepted the ice-cold beer the waiter brought.

Mitch had shown Larry the crib before they'd gone out on the links. "Thanks."

"So what are you going to do for a wood shop?" Larry took a long swallow before setting his beverage aside.

Mitch took a drink of his own beer. "I'm not certain. I'm putting everything in one of those storage units once I sell the house."

Larry reached for the bowl of peanuts. "That's because the condo's too small. You and Kristi need a house."

"The condo's bigger than my place."

"Yes, but a man has to have his own space, and houses are much better investments." Larry tossed a few nuts into his mouth.

"It's too much too soon. Wedding, baby and a move? Perhaps we'll think about moving early next year. We've already had enough changes for now."

"It took Kristi forever to buy that condo. I can't tell you how picky she is."

"I know." Mitch lifted his beer. Larry loved to give tons of unsolicited advice and Mitch was slowly learning to handle his father-in-law. "Which is why I don't want to rush. Getting it right is important. I would like to move only once more."

"That's understandable. I've been in the same house almost thirty-five years. Speaking of moves, I have news. You'll be moving into your new office next week. A room with a view."

"What?" Mitch put the glass down.

Larry grinned, delighted he'd surprised Mitch. "Yes. You're being promoted. Congratulations."

Mitch found himself temporarily speechless. While he'd returned to the Communications Department, his job title ranked him third. Larry hadn't followed through. Until now. "I wasn't expecting this." Then again, he'd never really told Larry not to do it. He'd said he'd think about it, and then life had gotten in the way. Larry had taken silence for assent. Mitch winced.

"This has nothing to do with you being my son-in-law. We've all been impressed with the work you've done. It's only fitting you be named a vice president. You've earned this spot."

Larry appeared to be unaware of Mitch's discomfort. "Don't look so surprised. I promised you that title months ago. I'm a man of my word."

"We've discussed this. I told you—"

Larry interrupted Mitch with a dismissive wave. "No need to be all self-righteous. We're men here. I've created a new position. It's vice president of Special Projects."

"What does that mean?"

"The Special Projects team will mainly be dealing with our corporate sponsorships. Those onetime things we underwrite—benefit dinners, plays, charity events…"

Mitch heard a noise behind his head, but the booth was high and designed to be private. The waiter brought drink refills.

"I thought of moving Brett back over when I split

the Communications Department, but really, there's no need. Kristi will remain VP of corporate communications. Your new title officially moves you onto equal footing with her and gives you half of her department. While she is on maternity leave, you will do her job. If she doesn't return, you will be vice president of corporate communications, as I promised. The entire division will be yours and the positions will be merged."

Mitch heard a strangled sound, and he rose slightly, peering around the corner of the booth. Kristi stood there, her face ashen. "Crap. Kristi."

She backed up a step, horrified by what she'd overheard. Larry stuck his head around and saw his daughter. "Kristi. Is your shower over? How was it?"

She looked at her father and then at Mitch. She'd started shaking her head. Her lips opened as she tried to form words, and then they quivered as tears ran down her cheeks. "You married me for my job. He gave you my job."

Mitch was on his feet. He knew what she'd overheard was damning, and that she'd never heard his side—it was all a big misunderstanding. "It's not like that. Let me explain. Damn it, Larry, I knew this was a bad idea."

"It's not personal. It's business."

But Mitch didn't care. Kristi had put her fingers to her forehead, whirled around and walked swiftly toward the door. "Kristi."

She didn't stop. "Kristi, wait!"

Mitch was aware that behind him Larry was now on

his feet, and that everyone in the bar was watching the scene unfold. He didn't care. He chased after his wife.

KRISTI COULDN'T BELIEVE what her father had done. Worse, Mitch had been a welcome party to it. So much for his loving her. All this time Mitch had been playing both sides. He'd struck a deal with her father, and then he'd made an agreement with her. He'd doubled down, hedged his bets, and won on all counts.

Special Projects? That position would disappear quickly, the moment she decided to stay at home like a good mother should. Her father was pushing her out of the company.

If Mitch really loved her... How could she believe that lie anymore? And if he did, well, this wasn't love.

She'd driven herself to the baby shower—as Mitch had arrived earlier with her father so they could play a round of golf. Well, Mitch could find his own way home.

Oh, why did relationships never work out for her? The moment she'd realized she loved Mitch, the rug had been yanked out from under her. She'd been leaving the bathroom when she'd decided to check the bar. The good news was that she had her purse with her. She fumbled for her car keys.

She heard Mitch calling her name, and quickened her pace. She did not want to talk to him. Not now. Maybe not ever.

Where were those keys? She rummaged through her

bag. Her car was close, and if she hurried, she could leave and go somewhere to think and—

Kristi's foot caught the yellow parking curb, and she tripped and stumbled forward, her entire body thrown off balance as she lost her shoe.

She dropped her purse, and instinctively put her arms down to protect herself. She heard more than felt the sickening crack as her wrist snapped. Then she landed on her stomach and screamed at the sudden, ripping pain before she rolled to her side. Her head hit the pavement and all went mercifully black.

Chapter Fifteen

To Mitch, Kristi's fall happened in unstoppable slow motion. But the moment she lay still, everything went into rapid fast-forward. Someone called 911. The baby shower guests arrived on the scene, and some began crying. Larry comforted Emma. Alison ordered everyone to stay back.

"It's going to be okay, sweetheart. The ambulance is on its way," Mitch told Kristi. She lay on the ground, her head in his lap. Her eyelids fluttered and she moaned.

His sister Kathryn, a nurse, leaned low. "She's coming around."

The ambulance roared into the parking lot, sirens wailing. Within minutes, they had Kristi loaded onto a gurney and whisked away. Mitch had never been in an ambulance before. He sat on the side bench seat as the paramedics monitored Kristi's and the baby's heartbeats. She'd regained consciousness, but she refused to look at him. Instead, tears ran down her cheeks, making Mitch feel like an insensitive, helpless cad.

The E.R. doctors at the hospital could see she'd

broken her wrist, but their biggest concern was that she had vaginal bleeding.

The baby took priority, and she was relocated to the maternity ward. A tall, dark-haired doctor around Mitch's age entered.

"Hi, Kristi. I'm Dr. Spencer Anderson. I'm one of Dr. Krasnoff's associates. She's out of town this weekend, so I'll be working with you today."

Mitch stepped out of the way. Dr. Anderson checked a few monitors, and moved to place a hand on Kristi's shoulder. "It appears that I'm the one who's going to be delivering your baby." He turned to the nurses. "Prep for C-section and get her to O.R. Stat."

Kristi's eyes widened. "What's wrong?"

"Your fall created some trauma. Given your history with spotting, we're going to play this safe." He addressed Mitch. "If you're staying, have the nurses get you some sterile scrubs and a mask. I'll meet you in the O.R."

With that, Dr. Anderson left the room, and several people flooded in. A few minutes later, Kristi had been whisked to the O.R. and was being prepped for surgery.

"I'm sorry," Mitch told her. She turned her head away from him.

"It's too soon," she whispered.

Dr. Anderson overheard her when he entered the room. "You're almost full term. Two weeks shy. Let's bring him or her into the world before we speculate that something's wrong."

They'd covered Kristi with protective drapes and sheets, and set up a sterilized barrier so that she couldn't view the operation. Standing, Mitch had a clear picture of everything, and he winced as the doctor began his incision.

"Tell me," Kristi demanded.

"It's like you see in the movies," Mitch offered, not wanting to go into detail.

"Don't faint on me," Dr. Anderson called to Mitch before giving the assisting nurse another instruction.

Then he was reaching inside and lifting up a small body. "You've got a boy," he announced as he passed him to a waiting nurse. Mitch heard suction noises and then a small cry.

Beside him, he heard Kristi's relieved sigh, and felt her warm tears as they ran down the side of her face and onto the pillow where he'd placed his hand.

"How is he?" he asked.

"Ten fingers, ten toes," the nurse replied, but Mitch knew that said nothing. The nurses working on his and Kristi's son had their backs to him, and he couldn't tell what they were doing.

"I'm stitching you up now, Kristi," Dr. Anderson said. "I promise you won't even see this scar. It'll be under your bikini line."

Kristi heard the door open and she turned her head. "Where's my baby?"

"We're taking him to the NICU," the nurse announced.

"Why?" Mitch asked.

"Precaution," she answered before the door closed.

Mitch saw Kristi's body tremble. "I want to hold him," she cried.

"That wrist isn't fixed," Dr. Anderson reminded her. He was still stitching her closed. "Let's get you all bandaged and checked out and then you'll be able to meet your son."

"I'm fine." That was Kristi's answer for every crisis, Mitch knew.

But even though Dr. Anderson was young, he was experienced. "You won't do your son any good if you can't hold him. I believe you're going to be sporting a cast."

"I don't think I like you," Kristi said.

Her declaration had the doctor laughing. "Yeah, I've heard my bedside manner pales next to Claudia's. Now, you're almost done here. However, I have to warn you, you're going to require assistance sitting up for a few days as your stomach muscles heal."

"I can't feel a thing," Kristi mumbled.

Dr. Anderson finished and pulled his mask down. "No, but you will. Dr. Krasnoff returns late tonight, so she will check on you tomorrow when she starts her rounds. The nurse is going to finish cleaning you up, and she'll get you where you need to go."

Kristi reached up and tugged on Mitch's arm with her good hand. "Find my son." He hesitated. "Go."

Mitch found the baby in the NICU. Looking in the window he could tell that the babies here were smaller. He had no idea which one belonged to him and Kristi.

"Can I help you?" A nurse had approached, probably noticing the scrubs he hadn't taken off.

"Mitch Robbins. My wife had a baby."

"And your wife is?"

"Getting her wrist bandaged. It's broken. She just delivered. Dr. Anderson did it by C-section."

"And her name?"

"Oh. Kristi. Kristi Robbins."

"Wait here." The nurse entered the NICU, and through the window Mitch watched her progress. He saw her speak with a nurse sitting in the center of five bassinet-style units, and then she returned. "Baby Robbins is sleeping."

"And? I have to go back and tell Kristi how he is. They didn't even let her hold him."

"Would you like to hold him?"

Mitch nodded. The nurse smiled sympathetically. "Then follow me."

HOURS LATER, a nurse named Sally finally wheeled Kristi into a maternity recovery room. "This is your home away from home," she said cheerily. "I'll be with you for the next twelve hours and I'll bring you some menus so you can pick out your meals."

"I want my son," Kristi said. She'd waited long enough, and her only consolation was that the NICU was on-site, and her baby hadn't been airlifted anywhere. She'd been told that she had quite a few visitors in the waiting room. As for Mitch, he hadn't come back.

Then again, she'd probably been difficult to find if

he had tried to locate her. She'd been to Radiology for X-rays and a CT scan. She'd been fitted for a cast on her wrist. She'd been declared concussion free, although her head pounded and she had a nice bump from when she'd hit it on the pavement. Her stomach felt empty, and was painful to touch.

"Have you seen my husband?" she asked.

"I believe he's in the NICU," Sally said.

"Can you please take me there? I still haven't seen my son."

Sally kept smiling. "Of course."

The first thing that struck Kristi about the NICU was the noise. Machines constantly beeped and mothers in rocking chairs tried to soothe their crying babies. Sally gave her a name tag. "This tells us who you are and what medical condition your baby has."

"What does my son have?"

Sally pointed. "I'm not sure, but that's your baby's pediatric nurse. She'll be able to tell you."

Sally wheeled Kristi forward, and she saw Mitch sitting in a rocking chair, a tiny bundle pressed to his chest. He looked up at her arrival. "How are you?" he asked.

Anger flared in her chest. He'd even taken holding the baby first from her. What else did Mitch want? Kristi held up her wrist, trying to stay on a safe topic. "I've been casted."

Mitch rose and brought the baby over. "Here's your mom," he told his son. He lowered the baby into her arms. "He's been waiting for you."

Kristi fingered the blanket. All she could see was a little red face. The rest of him was hidden beneath the small bunnies decorating the receiving blanket. But seeing her son's face, even with the oxygen tubes taped to it, was enough. He was beautiful, like his daddy.

Her vision blurred with tears. She was holding her son. "Why the tubes?"

"A precaution. His lungs weren't fully ready to work on their own, so this helps him breathe easier," the NICU nurse said.

Her son made a fishlike pucker before closing his mouth.

"He's feisty and strong and he keeps trying to remove his tubes. That's why we have them taped to his cheeks." The nurse moved to check on another baby.

Kristi's tears fell freely, and because her arms were full, Mitch found some tissue and dabbed her cheeks.

"He's so little," she said.

"Five pounds two ounces," he replied.

Nothing in Kristi's life had prepared her for this moment when every maternal instinct flowed into her. She was a mother. She and Mitch had created this little person, and she'd brought forth this life.

Raw, unconditional love. That was the only description for what she was feeling. She could do this. She was a mom. More tears sprung to her eyes.

"Hey, he's going to be fine. He's tough."

Like his father. Only, his father had betrayed her, and any future they had had been built on lies, the biggest falsehood of all being that there would be no more lies.

Her baby's nose wrinkled as a wayward teardrop touched his skin. She moved the blanket, seeing the white heart-monitor circles taped to his chest. Except for a diaper, her son was naked. The monitors and tubes made dressing him impossible.

The nurse returned. "It'll only take a minute to check him and you can have him right back."

Kristi's arms felt barren the moment she passed her child over. The nurse drew a blood sample by pricking the baby's heel. Kristi winced.

Mitch placed a comforting hand on her shoulder and she was too tired to shrug it off. "I've watched them work with him since I got here. Don't worry. He's getting excellent care."

"Is that your family?" the nurse asked, placing the baby back in Kristi's arms.

Kristi turned. Faces lined the length of the window. Her parents. Alison. Mitch's family. Everyone who'd worried and wondered what was going on.

Because of the monitors, she couldn't move closer, but Mitch turned her wheelchair so she could face them.

Her mother touched her chest, and her father held his wife close. Mitch's brother Logan gave a thumbs-up. Alison was nodding and smiling, as if saying good job.

Kristi was a mother now, and Mitch was her husband. For better or worse. Unfortunately, their marriage had been built on quicksand.

Chapter Sixteen

Two weeks later, Kristi and Mitch still hadn't talked about what had happened. She'd been at the hospital for three nights, and the baby had remained for another three days after that to ensure that he'd be strong enough to breathe on his own.

Mitch had been with her for the first forty-eight hours, until accusations that a recent sports promotion had deliberately targeted underage drinkers had required the skills of Jensen's new Communications VP.

She'd seen Mitch on TV, answering the allegations. He'd done an admirable job. Then, ever since he'd been called back to work, they'd barely seen each other. When he was home, he managed to give Kristi a wide berth while still helping her with chores and the baby. Every time he tried to broach the subject of his agreement with her father, she came up with an excuse to avoid talking.

"So when is everyone getting here?" Alison asked. She'd arrived early to prepare for tomorrow's baptism, which would be held at Mitch's family's church. She sat on Kristi's couch, baby Jackson Talbot Robbins in her arms. He was named for Mitch's and Kristi's grandparents, but they called him Jack—Jackson seemed like a big name for such a little guy.

The baby gurgled and Alison made a face and cooed. "You're such a sweet thing. It's hard to believe you'll grow up to color on the walls and drag mud inside."

Kristi laughed. "Carly's being adventurous again, I take it."

"Always. Jack is such a good baby. And you better be if I'm going to be your godmother," she teased him.

Kristi's pride and love overflowed. "Don't worry, he's always going to be a sweetheart. Unlike his daddy."

"You two need to kiss and make up."

"He took my job."

"You get a six-week maternity leave and you're going to take all of it or deal with me. You already look wiped out and Mitch has been helping."

"He does a great job," Kristi admitted.

"So start talking. Clear the air. For both your sakes and Jack's."

"What Mitch did was wrong. And now he's over my head in the chain of command. At least until I get back."

"Are you returning to work?"

Kristi sighed. "I haven't decided. I'm not even getting a full night's sleep, and since you swear that doesn't happen until Jack weighs at least eleven pounds, I have a long wait."

"You could use a break. How about I babysit tomorrow night after the baptism? Amazingly enough, my ex is in town to visit with his kids. You and Mitch can get out of the house and onto some neutral ground so you can talk."

Before Kristi could respond, the doorbell rang. Mitch, who had been in their finished basement, where he'd set up a home office, came up the stairs and opened the door.

"Neither of you should have to worry about cooking, so I brought a lasagna," Sue Ellen said as she entered. Mitch took the pan from her. "Now, where's Jack?"

"In here," Kristi called. Sue Ellen hurried into the living area.

"He's gotten bigger. Such a cutie." Arms already outstretched, she took him from Alison.

When the doorbell rang a few minutes later, Emma Jensen entered. Sue Ellen reluctantly shared.

Then, after another round of holding, Kristi fed Jack and put him in his crib so they could discuss tomorrow's baptismal ceremony. Mitch's brother Nick would be the baby's godfather, and Alison would serve as godmother.

"Did you put that lasagna in the oven?" Sue Ellen asked as Mitch stuck his head into the dining room over an hour later.

He arched an eyebrow. "That's for tonight?"

"Kristi, what are you and Mitch feeding us for dinner?"

Kristi shrugged. "Mitch has been planning most of the meals lately. Pizza?"

"Putting the pan in the oven," Mitch announced.

Sue Ellen was close enough so that she could pat Kristi's knee. "You'll have to train him a little more. He's clueless. I did the best I could, but now it's up to you. Oh, and while I'm thinking of it, I brought you something that I hope you'll like. Mitch." He leaned around the door frame. "Go to the car. I brought your baby albums."

Mitch didn't appear to be too excited about that. "Mom. No one wants to see those."

"Of course they do." Sue Ellen waved him out of the room. "After I had Lauri, I began getting duplicate prints of all the pictures I took. I kept individual albums for each of the kids so that someday it could be a keepsake for their children."

"That's a good idea. I still have Kristi's albums at the house. Do you want them?" her mom asked.

Kristi hadn't ever thought about it. "Oh, I'm fine."

"Maybe a few pictures," Sue Ellen suggested.

"I can do that," Emma said.

"I'll show you how to make a scrapbook," Sue Ellen offered.

"That would be nice."

Kristi watched the exchange. It was interesting having another mother figure around, and one who could manage Emma, too.

"So we've settled on white lilies and blue ribbon in the church, and the florist will deliver those," Alison said, directing the subject back to the real reason everyone was here.

"That's right," Sue Ellen said. Kristi shot Alison a grateful glance.

"But there is so much more left to do," Emma reminded everyone, and they got back to work. Mitch set the photo albums down on the coffee table, and disappeared to the basement again.

The women stopped only to eat dinner, and by 7:00 p.m. everything for the next day was finished. "Done?" Mitch asked. He came upstairs just as they were getting to their feet and stretching.

"Yes. It's going to be lovely," his mother announced.

"I think you'll be pleased," Emma added. "I am."

"I'm sure it'll be wonderful. I saw Kristi plan enough events. She got all her skills from you," Mitch complimented his mother-in-law. Then he turned to his mom. "And after raising all of us, you can manage just about anything."

"Flatterer," Sue Ellen said.

"Kristi, I have to go. Who knows what your father's gotten into while I've been gone." Emma hugged her daughter.

"I'll walk you out," Mitch offered.

Sue Ellen winked. "And while he's out, I have a naked baby picture to show you."

Mitch's mom went into the living room and picked up one of the photo albums. She flipped two pages. "Here. Take a look."

At that moment, Jack began to wail. "I'll get him." Alison got up.

"Okay," Kristi replied as she and her mother-in-law sat on the couch. In the photo Mitch was lying stomach down on a shaggy white throw rug. He'd lifted himself onto his arms, and laughed for the camera. "That's cute," Kristi said.

"I knew he was going to be a heartthrob even back then. But don't worry, he's only had eyes for you."

Yeah, because her dowry was a vice-presidential position. Her father had even had all her e-mail rerouted to his in-box. She pushed her anger aside. It wasn't Sue Ellen's fault.

"Speaking of pictures, the ones we took at the hospital were in today's mail. Mitch and I got you copies. I can't believe I forgot. I had some to give my mother, too," Kristi said. She rose, went to the kitchen and took the envelope she'd prepared off the desk.

She returned to her seat and pulled the photos out. "We got you a five-by-seven and some wallet-size shots."

"That's perfect. Jack will hang in the hallway next to Jane." Sue Ellen took the pictures and studied them. "He is such a darling. He looks just like Mitch did. Oh, a little smaller, but almost identical. Babies are so adorable, aren't they?"

Mitch walked over and his mother removed the photo from the album and held both out, side by side. "If I didn't know better, I'd swear this was you. Jack even has your ears." She smiled warmly. "You are all so lucky. Such a loving family."

Such a lie, Kristi thought.

"I should be going," Alison said, as if sensing the growing tension. "Mrs. Robbins, can I walk you out?"

"Oh, my, it is getting late." Sue Ellen replaced the baby picture, pocketed her photos of Jack and stood. "Let me hug my grandson again before I go."

After a cooing session, she reluctantly passed the baby to Kristi, who put the bottle in Jack's mouth. Alison followed Mrs. Robbins out, and a few seconds later, only Mitch remained in the room.

He reached for Jack, but Kristi clutched him to her. "I'll put him in his crib myself."

"I was only trying to help."

"You've done enough," Kristi replied, strapping Jack into his bouncy seat instead. She'd put him in the crib later.

"You have to let this go," Mitch told her.

"Why? You have my job. You know my father isn't going to want me back."

"It's not about the job. It never has been."

"Please. I'm not stupid. Every guy I ever dated seemed to either want something from me or find me lacking. You fit into the first category. You just hit the mother lode by marrying me."

"I love you. I want us to be happy," Mitch protested.

"Do you really think we can be like this?" She used one hand to flip open his baby book. The love that his parents had for each other was obvious in their eyes and smiles.

"Yes, I do believe we can be like that," Mitch said.

"I don't."

He exhaled his frustration. "Why not? What's so wrong with us?"

"Everything. You lied even after we said no more lies. You should have told me about the promotion."

"How many times do I have to tell you it's not about work?"

"Yes, it is. You want me to stay home and raise Jack, don't you?"

"That has nothing to do with—"

"If I stay home, you keep my job permanently. It's what my dad's been wanting this whole time and what you've been angling for. It's why you married me."

"You asked me to marry you. I said I'd be fine if we didn't get married." Mitch rubbed the back of his neck.

"Where else were you hoping things would go?"

"I don't know. Not here. I hate fighting and I don't want to fight with you. Not now, not ever. Kristi, I love you."

"How do I know what you feel for me is real? How can I trust anything you say after you conspired with my father to take my job from me?"

"I didn't take your job deliberately, but as you are on maternity leave, someone needs to do it and I'm the most qualified."

"Admit it, you like doing my job."

"Of course I like the job. I've always wanted this type of opportunity. But none of that matters compared to what I want with you."

"I don't believe you."

"You don't love me, either. You've never said the words."

"Well, that's because I don't."

He could see the lie written all over her face and it broke his heart. Lies kept coming between them.

"If you can't even be honest with yourself, how are we going to have a chance?" he demanded.

She made the protective gesture of covering her chest with her arms. "Maybe we don't. Maybe you should just go."

"Is that what you really want?"

"Yes."

"You're lying." He reached out to touch her arm, but she flinched and stepped back. He dropped his hand. "I'm going to go out for a while. We both need some space."

Her eyes widened. "Where are you going?"

"I don't know."

"Will you come back?"

"You told me to go. Now you want to know when I'll be back. What is it you want from me?"

A cloud of darkness settled over Kristi's face and the fire in her eyes died. "You said you'd never leave. Was *that* a lie?"

He couldn't reach her, not when she was like this and when his own control was so precarious. "We'll talk later, once we've both calmed down." He left quickly, before he could say anything to make matters worse.

KRISTI STARED at the door and wondered exactly what she'd just done. Why had she driven him away? Why had she fought with old tactics designed for failed relationships?

In his bouncy seat, Jack stirred and she bent to pick him up. "It's okay, sweetie," she told him. "Everything's going to be fine." She wondered if this was yet another lie.

"SORRY. I DIDN'T KNOW where else to go." Mitch stood on his sister's doorstep around nine-thirty. He'd driven around aimlessly since he'd left Kristi. He didn't know what to do, how to convince her to forgive him.

"Of course you should come here. I'm your sister." Maria shot her husband a glance and Paul left the room. "What happened?"

"Kristi doesn't believe I love her. She thinks I married her to climb the corporate ladder, and she won't listen to reason. I can't take it anymore."

"That's because you've never had so much to lose before. I know I've never been very supportive of your relationship with Kristi, but let's take a look at this from her point of view. You told me that every guy she ever dated dumped her. So she's probably got a bit of an inferiority complex. Then she has a great no-strings night with you, and gets knocked up. But instead of telling you, she keeps it to herself because she doesn't want to trap you. She just wants to be loved for herself."

"I do love her for herself. I have for almost three years. And I thought we'd gotten past all that. But she's never looked at me the same way since she overheard my conversation with her father. She won't believe me, no matter how many times I explain."

"Here, try this." Paul entered and handed Mitch a cup of coffee spiked with Irish cream. Mitch took a sip of the warm, soothing drink.

"Thanks," he said before Paul left.

Maria smiled. "It's Paul's favorite calm-down drink. I guess he figured you could use one."

"Is this how it is when you two fight?"

"Sometimes. Other times it's better, and there are times it's worse. But he's a good man. We love each other enough to work through things no matter how bad they get or how impossible they seem."

"The last thing Kristi did before I left was ask me when I'd come back. She said I promised not to leave her. Deep down, I'm sure she loves me. But she's afraid."

"Which is why you need to work things out. It doesn't matter how you both got here. It only matters where you go from here. You're going to have to forgive yourself, and her. And she will have to forgive you. Then you'll have to put it in the past and move forward. Is she worth it?"

"What?"

"A lifetime."

Scenes from his life flashed in his mind, as if watching highlight movie clips. Kristi in her red dress, dancing with him at the Christmas party. That same dress coming off. The meeting in the stairwell. Dinner at his place. Long discussions over the union negotiations. The night at her condo when she'd asked him to marry her. Standing next to her and saying I do. A honeymoon spent whale watching amid glaciers, with eagles flying overhead. He could hear her laugh, see her smile, feel the satiny smoothness of her skin.

"She's worth it," he said.

"Then you're going to have to figure this out."

"The grand gesture works," Paul said, entering the room and glancing at Mitch's coffee. Mitch put his hand over the empty cup, indicating he didn't want a refill. "I bought Maria a diamond tennis bracelet after I accidentally broke her porcelain vase, you know the one that was your grandmother's? I bumped into the table and it fell off and shattered."

His sister nodded. "I was so mad. I was pregnant and hormonal and I exploded. I felt so bad afterward, but Paul kept saying it was fine. And then a few days later I found a box on my pillow. He'd even written me poetry."

"She blubbered," Paul said, grinning. "She was putty in my hands."

"Oh, you," Maria said, and Mitch could tell how much his sister truly loved her husband. They were soul mates. He'd always thought he and Kristi were soul mates, too.

"He didn't need to buy me anything. The vase was an accident and really not that important. But the fact he accepted responsibility, even when it was really not his fault, said volumes about how much he loved me."

"Jewelry won't work. Not this time. Broken trust will take more to mend than a broken vase."

"The key is that the gesture comes from the heart. Maria loved that vase and she'd always longed for a tennis bracelet. You have to be willing to own the blame, even if you aren't guilty, and try to meet Kristi's needs because you love her," Paul advised.

"What if she doesn't believe I'm sincere?" Mitch asked.

Paul shrugged. "You convince her."

"Should I inflate the air mattress?" Maria asked. "It's probably best you stay here tonight. If you go home, you risk getting into another fight. Both of you could use some space. A night away won't make things any worse, and it'll give you some time to think. But make sure you call her and tell her where you are."

Mitch nodded. He didn't want to go home and get into another argument. That's why he'd left in the first place. He had decisions to make. Today had shown him he had one last chance. He loved Kristi. He loved his son. One more strike and he'd be out.

He couldn't let that happen.

By 3:30 A.M., as Kristi fed Jack, it was obvious Mitch wasn't coming home. He'd called to tell her he was staying at Paul and Maria's and he'd be home in the morning, but as she returned Jack to his crib, she realized she'd hoped he would change his mind. The condo felt empty without his presence, and that emptiness resonated within her.

She did love Mitch, and no matter how mad she was, she couldn't help wanting him near. But what a mess their relationship had become.

She stroked Jack's cheek, and he closed his eyes.

Funny thing was, as mad as she felt about Mitch taking over her job, she loved staying home. She didn't miss work as much as she'd thought she would. Every day Jack did something new and she didn't want to miss a minute. That big PR crisis Mitch had taken care of hadn't even raised her adrenaline the way Jack's cry did. Work had never given her the contented, peaceful feeling she had when holding her son.

She turned the mobile on and then ran her fingers lightly over the crib rail, remembering her joy when she'd first seen the crib. She'd experienced such a revelation—she'd loved Mitch. She'd gone to tell him, and her life had fallen apart.

Kristi flipped off the overhead light. A night-light glowed in the corner. She didn't want to return to her room and the big empty bed that would emphasize Mitch's absence. She sat down in the glider and eventually slept.

MITCH FOUND KRISTI in the nursery early in the morning when he returned home. She looked so fragile sleeping there, her hair down around her shoulders and her head tilted to one side. His heart broke as he covered her with a fleece blanket and slipped away without waking her or Jack.

Having showered at Maria and Paul's, Mitch only

had to change his clothes and get dressed. He left Kristi a note, and met Larry at the country club for their 7:00 a.m. tee time. He and his father-in-law were part of a foursome competing in a golf tournament. They couldn't get out of it since Jensen was the sponsor, but both men would leave early to get to the church for the noon christening.

"Hey, Mitch. Adam called and they'll be on the course in five minutes," Larry said.

Mitch readied himself. He could do this. He could say the words that had to be said. "Good, because I need to tell you something."

He and Larry stepped out of earshot. All around, caddies were putting clubs in golf carts. "What is it?" Larry asked.

"Kristi's not happy about my taking over her job. We had quite a fight about it."

Mitch saw their partners arrive. He only had a few minutes, tops, because they had to run on time today in order to be at the christening. "I need your help."

"Anything."

"Good." Lying on an uncomfortable air mattress had given him plenty of time to think. "Let me tell you how things go from here."

Chapter Seventeen

As Kristi readied Jack for the trip to the church, Alison sat in the glider and rocked her feet back and forth. "That's a beautiful outfit."

Kristi adjusted the lacy white baptismal gown. "Every Robbins baby since Mitch has worn it, including Jane. Now it's Jack's turn."

"How are you holding up?"

"Feeling stupid that I arranged a christening the same day as the big Golf for Leukemia event that Jensen always sponsors."

"Well, Mitch called you, right? Is he on his way home?"

Kristi nodded. "He only played nine holes, enough to put in the required appearance." She curled Jack into the crook of her arm and fingered the ruffled edge of the gown. "I don't know what to do."

Alison frowned. "You have got to snap out of this. You also need to talk to Dr. Krasnoff and make sure you're not suffering from postpartum depression."

"I don't think my feeling blue is PPD. I'm moody because once again my life is a big mess."

"Tell him you love him," Alison suggested.

"That's ludicrous. Why would I do that? Why would I make myself vulnerable after what he did?"

"Because, honey, honesty from this point forward is the only thing that's going to save your marriage. And you do love him. In fact, tell him today in church. Is there any better place to bare your soul?"

Jack's lips puckered. "He needs to eat," Kristi said.

"I'll go get his bottle." Alison headed for the kitchen.

As Kristi sat in the rocker, she heard the front door open. Mitch was home. She heard a few murmurs between him and Alison and then he appeared in the nursery doorway. She glanced up. "Hi."

"How are you?" His voice was soft.

"I'm fine."

He nodded. "We are going to work this out. I promise."

She looked at Jack, whose eyes were closing.

Mitch stood there as if waiting for a response. "I'll go change," he said after a few moments.

After Mitch left the room, Alison returned, carrying a bottle of formula. "I'm going to leave you two alone and meet you at the church. Talk to him."

But her mother called, and then it was time to go to mass. Kristi sat next to Mitch for forty-five minutes. To a casual observer, she appeared to be perfectly put together, as if nothing was wrong. She'd applied her makeup expertly, hiding the dark circles under her eyes. As she smiled for her family and friends, she wondered if this was a mask she'd have to wear for the rest of her life.

As MASS ENDED, Mitch touched Kristi's hand, and felt her tremble. He had to make this right.

He bided his time. After mass the church cleared of all but the Jensen and Robbins families and their closest friends. The priest began the christening with a prayer. Then there was a song, followed by a short, spiritual message. Mitch couldn't remember Jane's baptism perfectly, but he knew there was a little leeway in the structure until the actual anointing of the baby with water and oil—then the words were canon.

"Mitch, as Jack's father, would you like to say something?" Father Steven asked.

Mitch rose to his feet, and headed to the front of the church. His starched suit itched, a sure sign of nerves. He'd spoken with the priest over the phone early this morning, but other than that, no one knew what was in his heart or what he planned to say. The lectern was elevated, and once at the mic, Mitch faced everyone. The Robbins and Jensen families took up multiple pews.

Mitch drew a breath. Then he felt a light touch on his suit sleeve as Kristi put her hand on his arm. Those blue eyes he adored looked up at him. "Do you mind if I go first?" she asked.

He shook his head. What he had to say could wait, but he would say it. "No. Go ahead."

"Thanks." He switched places with his wife, and stood on the floor behind her. Her voice was loud and clear.

"Hi. Thank you for coming today. As you know, Jack is Mitch's son."

He couldn't see Kristi's face, so Mitch moved to stand in front of the lectern.

Kristi drew a breath and continued. "I didn't do things the way I was supposed to, and I don't want you to think that I married Mitch because of the baby, especially since our wedding was rather rushed."

As he watched Kristi, Mitch's heart swelled with pride. Her blond hair was pulled back and she'd worn a loose-fitting green dress; her body had lost much of the baby weight, but not the last few pounds. The sun filtered in through the stained glass, creating a halo effect. She was a beautiful vision, and he knew exactly what she was trying to do. She was setting things right and he loved her for it.

"On a day like today, when we ask God to watch over and bless this child, it's important that the family house be in order. That there are no more bombshells that could rip everything to shreds. That's why I'm standing here, baring my soul."

Her eyes caught his, and for a minute the rest of the church faded away. "Mitch, my entire life I've wanted a man who loved me for me. One who'd be my best friend, my lover and the father of my children. You've been all of those, and I'm sorry I hurt you by not telling you sooner. I hope you can forgive me."

In his portable car seat, Jack stretched his fists into the air and made a gurgling noise. He was starting to wake up. Alison adjusted his pacifier.

Mitch was aware that everyone in the church was waiting for his answer, including Kristi. Tears had formed in her eyes, creating a wet sheen. There really wasn't space for two at the lectern, but Mitch climbed the steps and made room. This was his wife. He loved her.

As Maria had said, it wasn't how they got here that mattered, it was where they went from here. Years from now he'd be old and gray, and hopefully holding Kristi's hand as his father was holding his mother's this very moment. The future was theirs to create.

Love indeed did conquer all, if you let it.

He took Kristi's hands in his, as he had the day they'd married in Emma's rose garden. Peace settled over him, and he smiled down at her, so overwhelmed with joy that he wanted to burst. His lips opened and he spoke from his heart.

"I promised to love and cherish you all the days of your life. That hasn't changed."

Her eyes widened and he tightened his grip on her hands. "Through better or worse, sickness and health, for richer or poorer, and everything else in between. I love you. We're a family. Forever."

The collected breath of the onlookers whooshed out as he drew Kristi into his arms and gave her a light kiss.

He felt her tremble. She was so strong, his wife, but her heart had been broken so many times before. Those experiences had left her vulnerable. Unable to believe. Afraid.

"I love you," he repeated as they drew apart, for really, those were the only three words that could heal her. "I'm the luckiest man alive. You are the world to me."

Her eyes moistened again. "And you me. I do love you. I do."

Her words arrived with an anguished cry, and Mitch used his body to shield her from their families. "I know."

He'd brought a handkerchief for the christening, and he removed the white fabric square from his suit pocket and wiped away her tears.

"You always believed I loved you, didn't you? You knew my heart better than I did," she said.

He found in himself a tenderness he'd never known existed. "You couldn't act the way you did and not love me. Then I found out about Jack and once I calmed down, I realized how lucky I was. I had you and I had a son. Not that I wouldn't have loved him. But he's ours. We made him together, and he'll always know he entered this world loved."

The priest had moved to the lectern steps and Mitch nodded at him. "Let's get Jack baptized," he said to Kristi. "I heard there's a lunch afterward, courtesy of your mom."

That brought out a tentative smile on Kristi's face

and, his hand secure on her arm, Mitch guided her down the steps. The priest said a few more words to refocus the event, and Kristi's tears dried. Soon everyone convened around the baptismal font, where Jack was christened. The commotion woke him, but he didn't cry once, although his nose wrinkled as water and oil anointed his forehead.

After the ceremony ended, everyone moved to the church basement, where Emma's caterer had outdone himself. There weren't any streamers. This time flowers and white tablecloths ruled the day, as did delicious food served on china.

Mitch kept Kristi close for most of the meal. He knew he should share, but selfishness won out. He'd never been so happy. He had it all.

But there was one last thing he had to take care of. He turned to Kristi between the main course and dessert. "I talked to your dad."

"Oh?"

"I told him that should you decide to return to work, I'll step aside. I've always maintained that I don't want your job."

Kristi glanced across the room, and, as if knowing the topic of their current conversation, Larry held up a champagne flute and smiled.

"You did that for me?"

He held her hands again and nodded. "Like I told you, it was never about the job. It's always been about you."

Kristi sat back. The caterer had covered all the ugly

brown metal chairs with pretty, white linen seat covers. "You don't want to be a vice president."

"I love being a vice president. But I don't want any job if it means losing you. I only went along with your father because I hoped I could turn these one-sided feelings of mine into a two-way street. I'd loved you for so long. But the love I have for you now is different."

"How's that?"

"When I first met you, my feelings were like puppy love, or a crush. Then the more I worked for you, the more I realized that you were my soul mate. But I thought you'd never see me the same way, and I resigned myself to being your friend and coworker. After we made love on the night of the Christmas party, I was ruined—I finally knew for sure how great things could be between us, but I thought I'd never get to be with you again. But none of my feelings went away. When we started dating, those feelings matured. I realized you truly were my other half, the person I wanted to spend the rest of my life with. And I knew that here." He touched his chest above his heart.

The joy Kristi experienced at that second was like a balloon that would never pop. He loved her completely. "I'm glad you believed in me. Even when I didn't know myself."

"Last night when I left you, I went straight to my sister's. Maria told me that all people are going to argue, but if you love someone, you work through it. You don't quit. And you forgive each other."

Wow. His sister had said that? "I didn't think Maria was my biggest fan."

"Maybe not at first, but she made me see the light. If you give her another chance, the two of you might become good friends."

Kristi surveyed the crowd, finding the table where Maria and Paul sat. Jane was on her mom's lap, silver spoon in hand. Maria saw Kristi and tentatively smiled. Kristi smiled back, and then turned to Mitch. "You've been right about everything else, so you're probably right about this, too."

"Don't give me that much credit. I've also been wrong about a great deal. I'm not perfect."

"You're close." She placed her hand on his cheek and he turned his head so he could kiss her palm. "Please don't ever leave me again. Not even for a night. I couldn't even sleep in the bed—it was too lonely without you."

He kissed her fingers. "Never. That air mattress was nasty, but I didn't want us to fight. I love you."

The words that had been so difficult were now easy to say. "I love you, too."

"I don't think I'll ever get tired of hearing that." Mitch removed her hand from his cheek as the photographer hired by Emma said he needed them for a minute. They were separated, and Kristi found herself next to her mom and dad.

"Happy?" her dad asked, sounding slightly worried.

Kristi didn't have to lie. "Very much so," she reassured him.

"That was a brave thing you did in church," Emma said.

"Thank you. I love him. I didn't want anyone to doubt it." Kristi paused and a wide grin split her face. "I'm in love. I'm happy. He loves me. We're a family. It took a while, but I got it all, didn't I? I told you to be patient and that I'd find my own way."

"Wait until you have a girl and you'll understand how a mother worries," Emma defended, but she was smiling.

Her dad puffed out his chest. "I believe I played an instrumental role in your good fortune. Admit it, my archaic ways found you a good husband."

"Larry, what did you do?"

Larry looked sheepish when he heard his wife's question. Up until now, Emma had been unaware of Larry's manipulations.

"Oops." He shot Kristi an I'm-in-trouble look and took Emma's arm. "It's a long story."

"We've been married a long time," she reminded him.

"Good, then you'll forgive me, especially since what I did turned out so well. Although, really, I think Mitch is the one who's been in control the whole time."

"Yes, Mitch made sure I'll get my job back," Kristi said.

Emma's eyebrow arched. "You took away her job?"

"Not exactly," Larry replied, leading his wife out of

earshot, probably so that Kristi couldn't dig him in any deeper.

Mitch returned and slid his arms around Kristi's waist from behind. She let her body sink against his. "What's going on?" he asked.

"My dad let it slip that he meddled and found me a husband. He's off to try to get himself out of the doghouse."

Mitch laughed. "Good luck to that."

Kristi watched the conversation begin. Her mom didn't appear to be too pleased. "She'll give him grief, but then she'll forgive him. She always does."

"As long as you always forgive me. Have I told you I loved you lately?"

"Not in the past few minutes."

His hands rubbed her stomach, and Kristi wondered how many children they'd eventually have. They'd have plenty of opportunity to practice. She had an appointment with Dr. Krasnoff next week, and hoped to get the green light for lovemaking. Until then, she had plenty of other ideas for what she was going to do with Mitch later tonight.

Sue Ellen interrupted the moment and brought her grandson over. "Let's take a picture of the three of you. I'm starting Jack's photo album."

She passed the baby over and lifted the camera. Kristi and Mitch held Jack between them and Mitch wrapped his arm around her.

Sue Ellen pressed the button and then showed Kristi the digital display. The photo had frozen them forever;

however, instead of facing the camera, both Mitch and Kristi had turned their heads. They were smiling at each other, the love between them obvious. And Jack, curled in his mother's and father's arms, appeared to be looking up at both of them. "Oh. That's perfect," Sue Ellen said, admiring the shot.

The picture had shown the truth. "It is perfect," Kristi agreed.

And she knew it always would be....

*Rancher Ramsey Westmoreland's temporary cook
is way too attractive for his liking.
Little does he know Chloe Burton came to his
ranch with another agenda entirely....*

That man across the street had to be, without a doubt,
the most handsome man she'd ever seen.

Chloe Burton's pulse beat rhythmically as he stopped
to talk to another man in front of a feed store. He was
tall, dark and every inch of sexy—from his Stetson to
the well-worn leather boots on his feet. And from the
way his jeans and Western shirt fit his broad muscular
shoulders, it was quite obvious he had everything it took
to separate the men from the boys. The combination
was enough to corrupt any woman's mind and had her
weakening even from a distance. Her body felt flushed.
It was hot. Unsettled.

Over the past year the only male who had gotten
her time and attention had been the e-mail. That was
simply pathetic, especially since now she was practically drooling simply at the sight of a man. Even his
stance—both hands in his jeans pockets, legs braced
apart, was a pose she would carry to her dreams.

And he was smiling, evidently enjoying the conversation being exchanged. He had dimples, incredibly
sexy dimples in not one but both cheeks.

"What are you staring at, Clo?"

Chloe nearly jumped. She'd forgotten she had a lunch
date. She glanced over the table at her best friend from
college, Lucia Conyers.

"Take a look at that man across the street in the blue
shirt, Lucia. Will he not be perfect for Denver's first
issue of *Simply Irresistible* or what?" Chloe asked with
so much excitement she almost couldn't stand it.

She was the owner of *Simply Irresistible,* a magazine for today's up-and-coming woman. Their once-a-year Irresistible Man cover, which highlighted a man the magazine felt deserved the honor, had increased sales enough for Chloe to open a Denver office.

When Lucia didn't say anything but kept staring, Chloe's smile widened. "Well?"

Lucia glanced across the booth at her. "Since you asked, I'll tell you what I see. One of the Westmorelands—Ramsey Westmoreland. And yes, he'd be perfect for the cover, but he won't do it."

Chloe raised a brow. "He'd get paid for his services, of course."

Lucia laughed and shook her head. "Getting paid won't be the issue, Clo—Ramsey is one of the wealthiest sheep ranchers in this part of Colorado. But everyone knows what a private person he is. Trust me—he won't do it."

Chloe couldn't help but smile. The man was the epitome of what she was looking for in a magazine cover and she was determined that whatever it took, he would be it.

"Umm, I don't like that look on your face, Chloe. I've seen it before and know exactly what it means."

She watched as Ramsey Westmoreland entered the store with a swagger that made her almost breathless. She *would* be seeing him again.

Look for Silhouette Desire's
HOT WESTMORELAND NIGHTS
by Brenda Jackson,
available March 9 wherever books are sold.

Devastating, dark-hearted and...
looking for brides.

Look for

BOUGHT:
DESTITUTE YET DEFIANT
by *Sarah Morgan*
#2902

From the lowliest slums to Millionaire's Row...
these men have everything now but their brides—
and they'll settle for nothing less than the best!

**Available March 2010
from Harlequin Presents!**

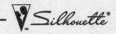

SPECIAL EDITION

FROM *USA TODAY* BESTSELLING AUTHOR
CHRISTINE RIMMER

A BRIDE FOR JERICHO BRAVO

Marnie Jones had long ago buried her wild-child impulses and opted to be "safe," romantically speaking. But one look at born rebel Jericho Bravo and she began to wonder if her thrill-seeking side was about to be revived. Because if ever there was a man worth taking a chance on, there he was, right within her grasp....

Available in March
wherever books are sold.

Visit Silhouette Books at www.eHarlequin.com

SSE65511

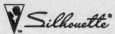

REQUEST YOUR FREE BOOKS!
2 FREE NOVELS PLUS 2 FREE GIFTS!

HARLEQUIN®

American ★ Romance®

Love, Home & Happiness!

YES! Please send me 2 FREE Harlequin® American Romance® novels and my 2 FREE gifts (gifts are worth about $10). After receiving them, if I don't wish to receive any more books, I can return the shipping statement marked "cancel." If I don't cancel, I will receive 4 brand-new novels every month and be billed just $4.24 per book in the U.S. or $4.99 per book in Canada. That's a saving of close to 15% off the cover price! It's quite a bargain! Shipping and handling is just 50¢ per book in the U.S. and 75¢ per book in Canada.* I understand that accepting the 2 free books and gifts places me under no obligation to buy anything. I can always return a shipment and cancel at any time. Even if I never buy another book from Harlequin, the two free books and gifts are mine to keep forever.

154 HDN E4CC 354 HDN E4CN

Name	(PLEASE PRINT)	
Address		Apt. #
City	State/Prov.	Zip/Postal Code

Signature (if under 18, a parent or guardian must sign)

Mail to the Harlequin Reader Service:
IN U.S.A.: P.O. Box 1867, Buffalo, NY 14240-1867
IN CANADA: P.O. Box 609, Fort Erie, Ontario L2A 5X3

Not valid for current subscribers to Harlequin® American Romance® books.

Want to try two free books from another line?
Call 1-800-873-8635 or visit www.morefreebooks.com.

* Terms and prices subject to change without notice. Prices do not include applicable taxes. N.Y. residents add applicable sales tax. Canadian residents will be charged applicable provincial taxes and GST. Offer not valid in Quebec. This offer is limited to one order per household. All orders subject to approval. Credit or debit balances in a customer's account(s) may be offset by any other outstanding balance owed by or to the customer. Please allow 4 to 6 weeks for delivery. Offer available while quantities last.

Your Privacy: Harlequin is committed to protecting your privacy. Our Privacy Policy is available online at www.eHarlequin.com or upon request from the Reader Service. From time to time we make our lists of customers available to reputable third parties who may have a product or service of interest to you. If you would prefer we not share your name and address, please check here. ☐

Help us get it right—We strive for accurate, respectful and relevant communications. To clarify or modify your communication preferences, visit us at www.ReaderService.com/consumerschoice.